FIRST STEP TOWARD SCANDAL

She could hardly believe her eyes. She was in the bedroom of an inn, alone with Lord Fletcher Belden.

She could hardly believe her ears when he said to her, "Would it be asking too much of you to pull off my boots?"

"Pull off your boots?" she had to ask. "You want me to pull off your boots? Why? Don't your legs bend?"

"You *are* in my employ at the moment," was his reply. "So now, if you would please to come over here and pull off my boots so that I might get into bed, I should greatly appreciate it. Or would you rather I slept beside you with them on?"

And she did not want to believe what would happen next. . . .

MICHELLE KASEY is the pseudonym of Kasey Michaels, which is the pseudonym of Kathie Seidick, a suburban Pennsylvania native who is also a full-time wife and mother of four children. Her love of romance, humor, and history combines to make Regency novels her natural medium.

SIGNET REGENCY ROMANCE

COMING IN NOVEMBER 1990

Irene Saunders

Lady Lucinda's Locket

Vanessa Gray

Best-Laid Plans

Leigh Haskell

The Vengeful Viscount

A Difficult Disguise

Michelle Kasey

A SIGNET BOOK

NEW AMERICAN LIBRARY

A DIVISION OF PENGUIN BOOKS USA INC., NEW YORK

SIGNET
Published by the Penguin Group
Penguin Books USA Inc., 375 Hudson Street,
New York, New York 10014, U.S.A.
Penguin Books Ltd, 27 Wrights Lane,
London W8 5TZ, England
Penguin Books Australia Ltd, Ringwood,
Victoria, Australia
Penguin Books Canada Ltd, 2801 John Street,
Markham, Ontario, Canada L3R 1B4
Penguin Books (N.Z.) Ltd, 182-190 Wairau Road,
Auckland 10, New Zealand

Penguin Books Ltd, Registered Offices:
Harmondsworth, Middlesex, England

First published by Signet, an imprint of New American Library,
a division of Penguin Books USA Inc.

First Printing, October 1990
10 9 8 7 6 5 4 3 2

Printed in Canada

Prologue

When titled Britain went toddling off to do battle with Napoleon Bonaparte and his Grande Armée, it did it with stylish English panache (more than a few handy umbrellas to keep the rain off their uniforms) and a patriotic fervor liberally mixed with a healthy appetite for adventure, war being regarded in the way of a highly desirable romantic escapade.

But now, at long last, Napoleon was safely locked up on Elba, and the war was over.

The Prince Regent—Prinny to his friends and, increasingly, Swellfoot to his enemies—who had never spent a long night in the cold rain with an empty belly or fought deadly hand-to-hand combat with a relentless enemy, viewed the victory as the perfect excuse to indulge in his most favorite thing in the whole world: a party of truly monumental proportions.

London's organized and spur-of-the-moment festivities, which had begun early in the year, intensified in June with the arrival of the Czar, as well as that of Blücher, a hard-drinking man who fast became the favorite of John Bull (as the everyday citizens of the metropolis were called), Prussia's spartan King Frederick, Count Platoff, commander of the Cossacks who had so successfully harassed Napoleon throughout that man's ignoble retreat from Moscow, and a host of other luminaries Prinny was hell-bent to impress with his entertaining genius, his outlandish, specially designed military uniforms, and his social largess.

By the second week in June the whole of Regency London was operating at a fever pitch, the usual hustle and bustle of the busy city magnified a thousand times, which was altogether wonderful if a person was in the mood to be entertained.

For the hardened veterans of battles in Salamanca and Badajoz, like Fletcher Belden, who was at the moment propping up the wall in a very hot, very overcrowded ballroom as all around him overdressed men and giggling women cavorted in a frenzy of celebration, all this carrying-on was not only frivolous, it was fast becoming downright dull. Turning his back on the crowd, he sauntered into the card room to try losing his boredom in the bottom of a deep glass.

1

"Who'll buy my sweet lavender?" . . . "Hot codlins! Cherry-ripe!" . . . "Chairs to mind? Bring out your chairs!" . . . "Milk-o! Milk below!"

Fletcher Belden groaned once, rolled over onto his stomach, taking his pillow with him, and buried his aching head beneath the soft goose down.

"Cockles! Cockles an' mussels, alive, alive-o!" . . . "Old clothes, mum? Old clothes to buy!" . . . "Cockles!"

The pillow hit the floor with considerably less than satisfying force as Fletcher bounded from the bed and stormed to the brocade bellpull, yanking the inoffensive signaling device so pitilessly that it ended by retaliating, rudely separating from its anchor to collapse in a mantle around the broad bare shoulders of its attacker.

"Beck," Fletcher roared in an abused tone, fighting his way free of six feet of tasseled bellpull and putting on the burgundy banyan that had found a home on a nearby chair back in order to cover his nakedness. "Beck!"

The doorway to the upstairs hall of the Belden town house opened, admitting both the glaring light of day and a slight brown-haired man of much the same age as his three-and-thirty-year-old employer.

"You bellowed, Fletch? Good God! You look as if you've been ridden hard and put away wet. But it is good of you to be nasty once in a while; it reminds me of how much I didn't miss your sharp tongue while you were on the Peninsula."

Fletcher shot the man a smoldering look as he ran a hand through his tousled blond hair. "Oh, capital! Just what I needed—humor before breakfast. I'm surprised you stay with me, Beck, when you've obviously got such a brilliant future in comedy. Perhaps you should reconsider remaining in my employ and take yourself off somewhere to scribble a book. Lord knows everyone else has. George has done all right for himself, although it did bring him Caro Lamb, which can only be considered unfortunate. No, I imagine one Byron is enough for any Season."

"My, my," Beck said, crossing the room to stoop awkwardly and rescue the torn bellpull from the carpet, "we are in a mood this morning, aren't we? Have a bit too much fun last night, my friend? Don't tell me you didn't enjoy dinner at the Guildhall. Did the Grand Duchess Catherine of Oldenburg order the musicians to stop playing again? That would be too bad, as then you would have been left with little choice but to listen to all those dry speeches."

"Fifteen toasts, Beck. We were forced to drink fifteen toasts. I think Prinny has run mad. Poor old Blücher was under the table again, and stayed there for most of the night. It took everything I had not to join him."

"As I understand it, poor old Blücher is always under some table or other."

Fletcher ignored Beck's remark and walked to the window that faced the square, threw back the heavy draperies, and slammed the window shut. "There! Perhaps that will keep some of that cursed caterwauling outside, where it belongs. It's either that or I order every chamber pot in the house emptied into the street via the upper floors. I'm persuaded it would be easier to fall asleep in the midst of battle than to find uninterrupted slumber past dawn anywhere in Mayfair anymore. Why did I go to that ball after the Guildhall? I must be demented."

Beck, Fletcher saw as he turned about, had seated himself on the edge of the rumpled bed, his stiff left leg extended in front of him, and was peering at him intently. Fletcher waited for the other man to speak, for he was not so incensed that he did not know he was acting like a bear with a sore paw, and decided he would be wise to shut up.

"Would you like some coffee, Fletch? I'll have to leave you in order to summon a maid to fetch some now that you have succeeded in dealing a death blow to this poor, innocent thing"—Beck pointed out easily, holding up the bellpull and waving the tasseled end back and forth for Fletcher's inspection—"but if you promise me you won't do anything rash while I'm gone, I'd be pleased to see to it for you."

Fletcher sat himself down in a chair facing the bed, looked at the ragged-edged end of the bellpull Beck was waggling in front of him, shook his head, and gave a small, self-deprecating laugh. "Maybe you ought to use it to bind my hands before carrying me off to Bedlam. I'm afraid, you see, that I just might be losing my grip."

Now it was Beck's turn to shake his head. No one knew Fletcher better than he, who had been his boon companion since the two of them had been in short coats. Fletcher Belden wasn't insane. As a matter of fact, he was one of the most sane, best-humored men Beck had ever encountered, as well as one of the finest, which was why Beck, who could have risen higher in the world than man of business, sometimes valet, and general factotum to his friend, was more than content with his lot.

"You're just tired, Fletch," he said commiseratingly. "Think about it. You returned from nearly five years away in the war—having, by the by, distinguished yourself no end with your heroic service; healed your breach with Vincent Mayhew by marrying him off to the woman you'd succeeded in tumbling into love with in the space of a week, a mighty noble deed, even if it did break your heart for a while, and then threw yourself head over ears into a round of peace celebrations that could succeed in accounting for more casualties than the Great Fire. Of course you're tired. Who wouldn't be tired?"

Fletcher looked at Beck for a long moment, then smiled. "You know what, m'friend? I think you're right. You know what it is? I'm getting too old for all this to-ing and fro-ing. Besides, it's bloody wearing. Whigs don't go to the Cocoa Tree, Tories won't be seen dead at the St. James's. Brooks's is Whig to a man, and White's was known to be Tory, but took down its flag and now takes anyone, money being the most powerful politician of them all.

"The Czar is courting the Whigs, while Castlereagh and Metternich are publicly telling Swellfoot everything is fine and privately having a collective apoplexy at Alexander's revolutionary ideas. I'm telling you, Beck, you can't sit down to dinner anywhere and attempt conversation without feeling that you're playing chess, blindfolded. I've even considered scribbling small hints to myself on my shirt cuffs, so that I don't inadvertently start chattering away nineteen to the dozen about personal freedom or some other such progressive anarchy while supping alongside a Tory, causing the poor fellow to choke on his turbot."

"Writing on your shift cuffs? It's a good thing you haven't, Fletch," Beck interrupted amicably, "as I have a devil of a time as it is keeping a washerwoman, with all the help tending to princes and kings and deserting their old employers. Although there are many things I'd do in the name of friendship, I'll be damned if I'll scrub your cuffs for you."

"That's another thing. I am so heartily sick of all the royalty that's running about." Fletcher stood up and began to pace, his bad temper catching him on the rebound. "The Princess of Wales is giving everybody fits, reminding all who will listen and half who won't that she is related to nearly all of her husband's royal guests and should be included in the festivities even if she isn't living with the Prince, most probably in the hope she can wring a reconciliation—or at the least, a higher allowance—out of the business. Prinny goes about the town with his great bulk hunkered down behind the closed drapes of his carriage, whether through fear of the mobs or his wife is anybody's guess.

"I tell you, Beck, I am almost nostalgic over reminiscences of short rations and forced marches in mud to my knees. Upon recollection, it was easier and probably less dangerous than trying to run about in society without getting tripped up over some inadvertent *faux pas*. Yes, I think I have had enough." He stopped his pacing and turned to his friend. "Beck," he asked, suddenly feeling better than he had in weeks. "I've had a thought. How would you like to go home?"

"Home? To Grasmere? With the real festivities still weeks away? I've heard that Prinny is building strange palaces in Hyde Park for a grand celebration. Go home? Can we do that?"

Fletcher, his clear gray eyes twinkling, answered happily, "Yes, yes, yes, and who in blazes is going to stop us? Think, my friend. I have given up my commission. I'm no longer a lieutenant colonel. I'm a plain, private citizen again. Fletcher Belden, landowner, who has been gone from his estate for nearly five years—more if you count that Season in London before I left for the Continent. It's more than time I took myself home."

This was a moment Beck had been both hoping for and dreading. He went to the doorway and flagged down a passing servant to order hot water brought for the master's bath, then turned back to face his friend. "What about the many clothes you ordered, Fletch? You commissioned enough to outfit a regiment in anticipation of all those invitations that are cluttering up the mantelpiece downstairs, and less than half of them have arrived—the clothes, that is. The rest of them can't possibly be completed for at least another fortnight or more."

Fletcher was pacing again, but this time it was with excitement rather than frustration. "Clothes?" exclaimed the man whose impeccable attire was most favorably compared with that of the incomparable Beau Brummell. "Hang the clothes! I'll be busy today, going about bidding my farewells to people I shall genuinely miss, and offering regrets to a half-dozen hostesses for being called back to my estate on some business matter or other that the two of us will have to trump up between us. My clothes can run home after me or remain here, for all I care. I don't have any time to lose. I've already missed the mating frenzy of the lapwings. Remember how we used to lay on our backs in the deep grassy hills above Lakeview and watch the males do those great twisting somersaults high in the sky over our heads? God, Beck, who would have thought I should be homesick for a bird?"

Beck stopped in the midst of laying out three thick white towels for Fletcher's bath, knowing he had to bring up another subject, one he had been studiously avoiding ever since he had joined his employer in town. "And your aunt, Fletch. She'll be that pleased to see you again."

The quietly uttered statement succeeded in halting Fletcher— who had been mentally waxing poetic over the nearly forgotten black-and-white lapwings with their incredible flashes of bright green and purple when the sun hit their feathers just right—in his tracks. "My aunt? What aunt?"

Busying himself with unearthing three starched muslin cravats from a drawer—as it was always prudent to have extras close at hand if some misfortune should occur during the tedious job of tying the original to perfection, rendering the thing unwearable—Beck answered quietly, "What aunt you ask, Fletch? Why, your Aunt Belleville, of course. As far as I can recall, she's the only aunt you have."

"Aunt Belleville is installed at Lakeview? Have you been hiding something from me, Beck? Am I ill?"

Fletcher pressed his well-shaped hands to his chest in dramatic fashion, as if to be sure his heart was still ticking along in a normal rhythm. "Good Lord, I didn't know. I'm not dying, am I? I most certainly must be sickening for something. Ever since I can remember, that woman would swoop down on Lakeview whenever either Arabella or I turned up with the measles or some such thing. Sydney Smith must have known her personally, for his description of her kind in his *Peter Plymley* was Aunt Belleville to the life.

"He dubbed her sort the 'affliction woman,' as I recall—a long-in-the-tooth, near-penniless spinster, some distant relation of the family who would descend on us, bags stuffed full with various vile-tasting medicines and hideous slippers embroidered by her own hand, to establish herself in the house expressly to comfort, flatter, fetch, carry, and generally drive everyone into recovering as quickly as possible so that she might leave before we were forced into succumbing to the illness of the moment, if only in order to escape her cheerful ministrations. So, tell me, Beck, what terrible malady is about to strike me down in my prime? Don't coddle me, man, I can take it."

"You're not ill, Fletch, as well you know. Aunt Belleville's presence at Lakeview is in the way of an accident, actually. It was after Arabella's, um, you know," Beck explained haltingly, averting his eyes as he spoke of the death of Fletcher's only sister. "Aunt Belleville was there for the services, if you remember, and just before you rode off hell-bent to get yourself killed on the Peninsula, you told her she could stay on at Lakeview as long as she liked because you couldn't care less what she did. Aunt Belleville, well, Aunt

Belleville liked. As a matter of fact, she's been most happily in residence ever since.

"The old girl's done wonders with the herb garden, Fletch," he ended hopefully, for he had grown to like Aunt Belleville very much.

There was a knock at the door and two servants came in, lugging large steaming buckets of water that they set down in the center of the room before extracting a hip bath from behind a brocade screen in one corner and relocating it square in the center of the room.

Five minutes later Fletcher was in the tub, lathering his broad, liberally hairy chest. "Aunt Belleville," he mused, knowing full well that his deliberate silence on the subject had been driving Beck to distraction. "And you've known this all along, haven't you, Beck? Of course you have. You've been living at Lakeview; it would be dashed difficult to miss the woman. Did it never occur to you to ask her to leave?"

Beck, who had just finished giving Fletcher's new dark-blue Bath suiting a vigorous brush-up, turned toward the tub with a grimace. "I think Lethbridge is sweet on her, Fletch," he said by way of explanation, shaking his head.

Fletcher's right hand stilled in the action of lathering his left arm. "Lethbridge?" he asked, his shoulders beginning to shake as he thought of the tall, too-thin butler and man of all work who had been at Lakeview ten years before Fletcher was born. "Our Lethbridge? God, what a picture! After all these years, to have the redoubtable Lethbridge smote by Cupid's leveling dart. Now I know I must go home, if only to act as chaperon. Tell me, Beck, do people of their advanced years bill and coo, or are they more civilized?"

Beck picked up a thick towel and advanced toward the tub, his stiff left leg giving his slight body an awkward gait. "They don't do anything, Fletch. Neither of them will acknowledge the attraction. But I will admit, it is great fun to watch them speak volumes with their eyes when the other isn't looking. But she is your aunt, you know, and as oldest male, you're responsible for her good name. Maybe it's time you asked Lethbridge his intentions."

Fletcher flung the dripping sponge at his friend, who quick-wittedly ducked, and they both applied themselves to making up a rollicking, risqué limerick they would gift Lethbridge with upon their return to Lakeview, so that the butler could, if he were to have run completely mad since Beck last saw him, employ it to win his true love.

Exactly two hours past noon Fletcher was sauntering up Bond Street feeling much more the thing, his ivory stick dangling idly from his hand, his entire attitude one of elegant ease as he casually inspected his surroundings.

He had been to see his tailor, for contrary to the impression he would like to give, Fletcher did care very much for his wardrobe, which was why he did not patronize Stultz, who, as Beau said, made clothes, not men. Fletcher was gratified to learn that the judicious application of a few guineas had guaranteed that he would not be traveling home without the remainder of his purchases.

By the time he got to Piccadilly the crush of people was very great and growing rapidly, with street vendors plying their wares at the top of their lungs while barefooted urchins slogged through the streets, muddy from a recent rain, to beg coppers.

He quickly turned toward what he hoped would be the relative quiet of St. James's Street, any thought of a walk in Green Park forgotten. The disturbing noise of the dustman's clappers and the pleas of several old-clothes men wearing long greasy caftans and balancing towers of hats upon their heads as they lurched along reminded Fletcher of the headache he thought he had left behind after a satisfying luncheon of grilled ham and biscuits.

He had taken no more than ten steps when he saw a tooth-drawer plying his trade on a very vocal, puce-waistcoated customer who was clinging to the underside of a three-legged stool for all he was worth while the tooth-drawer dug in the man's mouth with a dirty instrument. Fletcher sighed, raising a handkerchief to his lips, knowing he was overreacting to what could only be termed an everyday sight, but he also knew he'd had his fill of London and was more than happy to be leaving it for the beautiful—and much more peaceful—Lake District.

"Corns! Here now, corns," a large dirty man brandishing a knife and scissors yelled, not three inches from Fletcher's left ear. "Corns to pick, guv'nor."

Fletcher turned to the man, his lids lowered halfway over his suddenly hard gray eyes, and intoned gravely, "Gentlemen don't have corns, my good man. Just as you don't have teeth."

"Jolly good, Fletcher," came a voice from behind him as the quack surgeon backed away into the throng of people lining the flagway in the hope the rumor they'd heard earlier was true and Blücher was to visit the area today. "Care to join me for a drink? I can't think why I believed I could get through this mass of unwashed on foot, but there you have it! The two of us should most certainly be better served to stop in at one of the clubs than to try to make it any farther without at least a dozen foot soldiers to carve out a path for us. Christ on a crutch! One can't help but wonder if Prinny knew what he was about when he started on this celebration business."

"Henry!" Fletcher turned around to greet Henry Luttrell, a man who had made a spectacularly successful career out of dining out, his quick wit and pleasing manner making him a favorite with hostesses throughout Mayfair, which was a very good thing, as the man had barely any fortune at all and the money he saved on food could then be spent on coal and other small luxuries. "Tell me something, Henry. Have you ever seen London in such turmoil?"

The two men fell into step, walking away from Piccadilly. "The better question, Fletcher, is whether I have ever really seen London. For my experience, the city on a fine day is like looking up a chimney, and on a rainy day, it is like looking down one. I can barely wait until all this nonsense is over and I allow Lady Holland to have me as her guest in the country for an extended rest."

Laughing, Fletcher remarked, "I can only hope she will be sufficiently flattered. You don't allow just anyone to feed you, do you, Henry?"

"I should say not! Ah, here we are, my favorite watering hole, as I have a good friend here who allows me to charge my libations against his personal account. Aren't you coming in, Fletcher? My treat."

Fletcher shook his head regretfully, for he truly enjoyed Henry's company, but explained that he had much to do before quitting London for Grasmere.

"Grasmere? Wordsworth don't live there anymore, does he?" Luttrell asked.

"William left Dove Cottage a few years past, yes, but Beck, my man of business, has told me William has moved yet again to a lovely home near Rydal, which is only four miles or so from Grasmere. But I have no fears about any adverse effect on his muse, for there is nothing unlovely about any section of the Lake District. I can't tell you how I am looking forward to getting back there myself."

" 'I wandered lonely as a cloud that floats on high o'er vales and hills, when all at once I saw a crowd, a host, of golden daffodils,' " Luttrell quoted dramatically, one hand to his heart. "William does have a way with words, doesn't he? Yet all I really know of the Lake District is that it is rumored to rain there at least five times a day. Ferdie Johnstone was there last year and he tells me he very nearly drowned, and would have if he hadn't had the extreme good sense to keep his mouth closed whenever he was out of doors. It's hard to believe, for I've never known Ferdie to have any sense at all."

Luttrell leaned forward to peer at Fletcher. "I hate to see you go, my friend. Are you convinced you need to see all this dubious glory for yourself? I could just as easily come by several times a day in my new yellow pantaloons and pour water on your head. It wouldn't be any trouble, no trouble at all. You won't even have to feed me."

* * *

By the time Fletcher was once more in his bedchamber, watching as Beck bustled about in the midst of packing for the removal to Lakeview that was planned for first light the next morning, Belden was feeling the least bit ambivalent about his decision to forsake London for the quiet of the Lake District.

He would miss his friends, friends like Henry Luttrell, if not the mad carryings-on of society, of that he was sure, but the lack of companionship was not at the heart of his unease. It was the return to Lakeview, to the place where he and Arabella had grown up, that worried him—perhaps even frightened him.

It had been five years since Arabella's suicide—five years and a lifetime of hurt and misunderstanding. Had enough time passed for him to be able to face her memory with fondness rather than horror and pain? And then there was the lovely Christine Denham, now the Countess of Hawkhurst and "quite desperately" in love with her husband.

"Women."

Beck turned to look inquiringly at his friend. "Did you say something?"

Fletcher gave a rueful laugh. "I was merely thinking out loud. You know, Beck, between my disastrous misreading of Arabella and my failure to win the one woman I thought I could love, I think that I would be doing the entire world a service if I should decide to stay at Lakeview indefinitely and try my hand at poetry or something. Heaven knows everyone else is writing reams about the Lake District these days. Look at Wordsworth—Henry Luttrell actually quoted him to me this afternoon. But, regardless, I believe I have sworn off women."

Beck closed the case he had just filled and shook his head. "You can't do that, you know. You're too pretty. Fletch, and the women all love you. Think of the hearts you would break if you vowed to lead a monkish existence. No, you'll be back in London within the year, and most probably on the lookout for a young beauty with which to set up your nursery."

Fletcher leaned back, considering his friend's words. "Maybe, but if I don't see another comely young female between now and then, I would consider myself a very lucky man."

Traveling slowly, driving his curricle ahead of a coach containing Beck and a small mountain of baggage, Fletcher did not reach Lakeview until an hour before dusk four days later. The weariness brought on by long hours on the road lifted from his shoulders as he reined the pair of bays at the top of a small rise and looked down on his home.

Built of stone, as were most of the homes in the area, Lakeview had been in his family for twelve generations. His holdings in the center of the thirty-five-mile-square Lake District were not vast, but they contained some of the best pastureland in the vicinity, and Lakeview's production of milk, cheese, and wool had provided a considerable fortune that continued to increase over the years.

As the horses stamped, impatient to be moving again, Fletcher looked down the curve of the narrow lane, past the wide expanse of flower-strewn pastures to his holdings. His house, partially hidden by trees from this angle, rose to a full three floors, with wings jutting off either end. A large place to ramble about in alone, he thought; then he smiled as he remembered that Aunt Belleville was in residence. Perhaps thirty rooms were not enough.

His gaze slid to the barn and stables, which were located several hundred feet away from the house, and he smiled again. It was there, in the stables, that he and Beck had spent some of their happiest moments. Even after Beck's hunting accident, when he could no longer ride, the two of them had spent long hours currying the estate's horses and learning how to spit under the tutelage of one of Lakeview's grooms.

Fletcher felt a momentary pang of sorrow at the years he had spent away from Lakeview, but he was not the sort to linger overlong on matters that could not be changed. It was enough that he had learned from his mistakes. He had been Arabella's guardian for the last years of her life—and he had failed her. That was a fatal mistake he would not make again.

"Because I won't be anybody's guardian ever again—not that I can see a reason for anyone to ask me to be," he said out loud, one of the bay's pricking up its ears, as if on the alert for further orders from its master.

How long Fletcher would have sat at the crest of the small hill he did not know, but suddenly, without warning, the bright sun was lost behind a cloud, and the rain Henry Luttrell had spoken about so glibly came pouring down, effectively shaking Fletcher from his reverie.

He gave his horses the office to start and tooled the curricle down the lane, bypassed the drive that led directly to the house, neatly feather-edged the corner of the barn, and headed into the stable yard, preferring the team to be shifted to the dry stable as soon as possible. He, Fletcher thought, had been wet before, and he hadn't been pulling a curricle all day.

"You, boy, go to their heads, if you please," he called out to a slightly built black-haired youth he espied sitting just inside the open door of an empty stall, perched at his ease on an overturned bucket, safely out of the rain. He reined his pair to a halt. "Come on now, a little rain won't hurt you."

The groom shot him a darkling glance and remained where he was, a long piece of straw stuck in the corner of his mouth. "If it won't hurt me, then it stands to reason it won't hurt you either. I work for Fletcher Belden—not you."

"I am Fletcher Belden, boy," Fletcher announced, lightly hopping down from the seat and taking hold of the bridle of the gelding closest to hand. "And you'll be out of a job and sleeping under a sheep if you don't step lively."

"Sure you are," the groom said with great sarcasm, remaining precisely where he was. "And I'm Napoleon, lately escaped from Elba."

"Insolent puppy, aren't you? Where is Hedge?" Fletcher asked tightly. "I left him in charge of the stables, but I don't remember giving him office to hire smart-mouthed fools."

Fletcher was secretly pleased to see the color drain from the youth's face as the groom hopped to his feet so quickly the bucket toppled with a hollow crash. A moment later the youth was working at releasing the bays from their harness, droplets of rain running down his freckled, upturned nose.

Obviously throwing out Hedge's name had served to

prove his own identity. Fletcher's smile faded as he decided it was rather lowering to think he had been proven legitimate only because of his knowledge of the former jockey whom he had taken in ten years ago. His employees should know him by sight, as he should know them.

Not only that, but the youth's insolence had made it evident that, indeed, Fletcher had been away from home too long. It was one thing to leave Lakeview in Beck's capable hands, but it was quite another to believe that his estate could be run entirely without the guidance of its owner.

"My traveling coach will be here within the hour," he told the groom, suddenly eager to get to the house, his mind already on the reception he would receive there. He certainly hoped it would be warmer than the one he had gotten from this cheeky employee. "See that the stables are ready for another six horses, as I've brought two riding horses with me."

"I'll tell Hedge, then," the groom said, walking away, leading the two horses behind him. "If I can find him."

Overhearing the groom's last grumbled remark, Fletcher laughed aloud. Now he knew he was home. "Look inside the large cabinet at the back of the tack room. That's where Hedge always goes to recover from his bouts with demon liquor."

The groom turned his head about swiftly and Fletcher was momentarily taken back by the quick intelligence he saw in the lad's clear green eyes. "So that's where he slinks off to. I'll do that," he said. "Thank you, sir. I hadn't thought to look there. And, um, welcome home, sir."

"What's your name, boy?" Fletcher asked abruptly, thinking to begin his campaign to reclaim Lakeview for his own.

"It's Billy, Mr. Belden, sir," the groom said, his small chin lifted almost defiantly.

"Billy," Fletcher repeated, wondering how a junior groom had come by such clear, unaccented English. "And do you have a last name, Billy?"

The question seemed to startle the youth. "A last name? Why do you want to know?"

"Why shouldn't I know?"

The chin lifted yet another fraction. "No reason, I suppose. It's Smith," the groom answered shortly. "Billy Smith."

"Of course it is," Fletcher agreed silkily as the rain stopped, just as abruptly as it had begun. "I think I knew that even before you said it. I'll see you again, Billy Smith, and we will talk again."

And with that, Fletcher turned and walked toward the house, wishing Beck was with him, as he was willing to lay odds the brazen young groom was pulling a face behind his back.

2

"Well, fiddle-de-dee," Billy Smith hooted with a dismissive shrug as Fletcher Belden disappeared around the corner of the stable. "Idiotic fop. One more cape on that ridiculous white driving cloak and his shoulders wouldn't fit through Lakeview's front door. And those absurd boots! Whoever saw such silly long tops on a pair of boots? I wouldn't want the polishing of them, that's for sure."

As soon as the derogatory words were uttered, Billy gasped, suddenly sick with apprehension, and looked about, hoping against hope that no one had heard. Then he relaxed as it became obvious that no one had.

After all, "fiddle-de-dee" wasn't exactly an everyday expression for a groom, a fact that could be overlooked when one considered the possibility that Billy Smith might not have been born into this world already cut out to be a rousing success as a junior groom. As a matter of fact, as Fletcher Belden had already made clear he suspected to be the case, the Lakeview boy probably wasn't even named Billy Smith.

Yes, in retrospect, Smith had been a poor choice, but as Hedge (bless his drunken, uninquisitive nature) had never asked for a surname, the question—or the need to be prepared with an answer—had never arisen before the so handsome, so infuriating Fletcher Belden had asked.

"Higgenbottom," Billy said aloud, belatedly struck with inspiration. "Higgenbottom would have been much better—or Perkins, or Clark, or even Fitchcomb. A hangdog look, a toe stubbed in the dirt, and a mumbled 'Uh, sir, I dunno,' would have been infinitely better. Anything but Smith!"

It was most depressing, as an active imagination had never failed Billy before Fletcher had driven pell-mell into the stable yard—and it was about time he had shown up!—to make imperious demands and ask a half-dozen stupid, unnecessary questions.

Yet luckily—or unluckily, depending on precisely whose luck was being considered in the matter—the maddening Fletcher Belden hadn't stumbled onto a snippet of knowledge even more damning to the junior groom.

In point of fact, all carefully contrived outward appearances to the contrary, Billy Smith was guilty of a lie infinitely more damning than that of merely furnishing his employer with a patently false name. For, horror of horrors, the young groom was not a he at all. Billy Smith was a she!

The rough-woven breeches and long, loose-fitting tan smock she wore, combined with her slight, short figure, boyish haircut, and not entirely feigned rough-and-ready demeanor, had made easy work of fooling the frequently-in-his-cups Hedge into believing he had hired a stripling lad to do his dirty work for him around the stables—while he, Hedge, could then attend to more important duties, which had quite a bit to do with depleting as much of Fletcher Belden's stock of carefully laid down brandy as possible before that good man's return to Lakeview.

The young groom, whose true identity she had taken such great pains to hide, now knew that pulling the wool over Hedge's bleary brown eyes and keeping the inquisitive Fletcher Belden unaware of her gender were tasks no more alike than chalk and cheese, and she would have to be awake on every suit from this moment on if she hoped to achieve her considered objective without being unmasked, chastised, and sent back home to the truly terrible fate she was doing her utmost to escape.

As she stood on a stool and ran a brush down the smooth flank of one of the splendid bays she had unhitched from the curricle, Billy closed her eyes and conjured up the sight of Fletcher Belden as he had tooled the magnificent equipage into the yard. His skill in handling the ribbons impressed her in spite of herself, although his first command to her had not been the sort to engender warm feelings of friendship. How dare he command her to come out in the rain? Wasn't it enough that he was already wet?

Billy chuckled at her own arrogance and stupidity. Why shouldn't he order her outside, for pity's sake? She was his employee, wasn't she? She ate his food, got to exercise his horses, slept on clean straw in his stable, and pocketed his money. Why shouldn't he expect her to get wet for him?

"Of course, if he knew I was a lady, he wouldn't have asked it of me," she reasoned charitably, hopping down to move the stool to the other side of the horse and continue brushing the animal. "If I wish to keep my identity hidden, I shall have to swallow my stupid pride and take more care to act like a lad than a lassie. The next time Belden crooks his little finger in my direction, I shall run hotfoot to his aid, tugging at my forelock and gritting my teeth so that I don't read him a lecture on proper behavior, even if I should feel as if I am going to have a spasm. And I shall have to begin cultivating cruder English as well, as I'm sure it was my prunes and prisms grammar that had him looking at me as if he could see straight through my disguise."

That decision made, Billy turned her full attention to the horses, which she knew were prime bits of blood and bone deserving of only the best treatment, and made short work of settling them in their new stalls. Just as she was about to attend to the tack, which looked in sore need of an introduction to a polishing cloth, a high, whiny voice startled her into dropping one of the bridles.

"Lord luv a bloomin' duck, boy. The master's 'ome, ain't 'e? Does yer wants us both turned off, yer brainless looby? Oi ain't goin' back ter Piccadilly 'cause yer ain't gots the wits a bloomin' ox wuz born with, Oi ain't. It ain't 'ealthy fer the likes o'me there. Why in bloody 'ell didn' yer fetch me?"

Billy sniffed her disdain and consciously coarsened her speech. "Ha! Fetch you, is it? That's easier said than done. You're a slippery piece of goods, Hedge, when you want to be, and you want to be more often than like. It wasn't worth my trouble. But Mr. Belden's coach will be arriving soon, with two more horses just for you."

Hedge was a bandy-legged, no-longer-young ex-jockey. He had been forced to seek an early retirement from a lackluster career on the track by a horde of unhappy bettors to whom he had promised a winner, only to end up a lowly fifth in a race everyone but his mount had known to be fixed. He now walked up to stand nose to nose with an unrepentant Billy. Sticking out his bewhiskered chin and narrowing his eyes, Hedge looked his assistant up and down, then spat exactly one inch away from Billy's left boot—for, although Hedge had never been a very good jockey, he was a prime spitter. "An' since when is yer the one givin' the orders 'round 'ere, eh, boy?"

Billy turned her head, trying her best to get away from the smell of stale brandy that had slammed into her face with the force of a slap. "I wouldn't think to give you orders, Hedge," she told him, daring to back up a pace so that she could inhale without fear of becoming intoxicated on the fumes.

"Oi should 'ope not, yer filthy little beggar," Hedge stated emphatically, groaning aloud after nodding his head a mite too vigorously, for he had the very devil of a headache.

"It's only that Mr. Belden told me he's bringing along two horses just for his own pleasure, and I thought you'd want to have charge of them. I'll take the four coach horses. Unless you want them?"

Hedge stuck the tip of his tongue against the inside of his left cheek. "That makes eight 'orses," the groom said at last, having struggled to do the arithmetic in his head—or, as Billy supposed, by using the tip of his tongue to total the numbers by counting against his teeth. "With the five we already got, we're gonna be busier than a two-penny whore on 'oliday. 'Ow many is that exactly, anyways?"

"It's thirteen, Hedge," Billy supplied helpfully when it looked as if this further bit of addition was beyond him—probably because she already knew he had no more than ten teeth left in his whole head.

"Thirteen! Are yer sure, boy? Oi doesn't loik that. Oi doesn't like that at'al. Oi'd as soon 'ave a week long ragin' rumpus in m'bowels than 'ave such a sorry number livin' 'ere in the stable with us."

Billy bit her bottom lip to keep from smiling. Oh, the wealth of colorful language she had learned from Hedge's lips in her two months at Lakeview! It was a great deal more interesting than anything her endless procession of governesses had ever taught her, that was for certain.

So, Hedge was superstitious, was he? She'd have to remember that. "It's seventeen, actually, if we count the gelding, the mares, and the pony for Miss Belleville's dog cart," she supplied helpfully as Hedge was looking more than a little nervous.

Hedge slapped his young helper on the back with enough enthusiasm to send Billy reeling against a corner of the stalls. "So it is! Yer a regular right 'un, Billy boy, fer pointin' that out. Oi wuz a mite scared there, Oi has ter tell yer, but we'll be all right an' tight now. Seventeen—'ow 'bout that! Four more'n bad luck is good luck, right? Now look lively and gets yerself up ter the 'ouse ter 'elp with the baggage. Oi thinks Oi 'ears the coach comin'."

Billy, a firm believer in omens herself, as long as they were good omens, ran to do Hedge's bidding, her heart light once more.

Fletcher walked out onto the wide, curved portico that bordered the gravel drive and looked down the short flight of steps to where his friend was laboriously climbing out of the coach, his stiff leg extended in front of him.

"Ah, Beck, I heard a coach and prayed it would be you. None the worse for the ruts we met up with some five miles back, I trust? I've been missing you terribly, you know. I've been home for an hour with no one but a cheeky groom and straitlaced Lethbridge to welcome me, as dear Aunt Belleville seems to be out and about somewhere."

"She isn't here, then?" Beck responded, secretly pleased that he had been in time to act as a cushion between aunt and nephew.

"Don't look so delighted, my friend. Although it pains me most grievously to tell you, I fear she's up to her old tricks, visiting the sick or some such thing, and I have been waiting with bated breath to hear your opinion on the matter. Do you think it's fair, Beck, to allow her to do so? I mean, I would have thought being ill to be unlucky enough in itself, without having to be burdened with my aunt's ministrations as well, wouldn't you?"

Beck pushed away the coachman's helping hand, as he did not like being reminded of his ungainly appearance when trying to do things a moderately intelligent monkey could accomplish with relative ease. "She nurses them, Fletch. You act as if she visits the ill only to help measure them for the undertaker," he said once he was standing firm on the drive, brushing at his dark coat in order to rid himself of some of the road dust it had accumulated on the trip from the inn they had left that morning. "And, remember, Fletch, you promised to be good. Lethbridge might hear you, and I'd hate to see the old fellow go into a decline because you've been making jokes about the love of his life."

Fletcher waited until his friend had mounted the steps before exaggeratedly bowing in Beck's direction. "Forgive me, I beg you. I shan't do it again, as I like Lethbridge as much as you do—as much, I daresay, as anyone can, given the man's disposition. I'm nothing but the lowest of ramshackle creatures, without the faintest hint of how I should go on. Please, Beck, will you agree to become my mentor, pointing out the pitfalls of dealing with the love affair between my aunt and my butler without injuring either of their sensibilities? I should be ever so grateful for your assistance, truly I would."

Beck stood back, sniffing. "Point out the pitfalls for you, is it? Why? Just so you can be sure you haven't missed any of them?" He shook his head. "I don't know. I think maybe you shouldn't have left London, after all. It might have been better if you had remained there until all the frisk was out of you. You've been at Lakeview for less than an hour and already you are planning ways of driving its inhabitants to distraction."

"All the way to distraction, dearest Beck? I hadn't thought I should like them to go that far. But if you say so . . ." Fletcher shrugged, taking Beck's arm. "You're right, of course, but then, you're always right, aren't you? Tell me, does it ever depress you—being right, that is? It depresses me terribly, you know. I had already promised myself I would be good, but my first sight of the yellow saloon drove all my good intentions out of my head."

"What's wrong with the yellow saloon?" Beck asked worriedly as the two men entered the house. "It was fine when I left it three months ago to make things ready for you in town."

Fletcher smiled, a single, slashing dimple showing in his right cheek. "That's because it was yellow when you saw it three months ago, I should imagine."

"What?" Beck stopped dead, to gape at his employer.

"Yes, you may stare. Lord knows I did. But to continue. It was a perfectly lovely yellow: soft, creamy, and extremely soothing to the soul. But, alas, it is purple now. I don't like purple, Beck, not above half. Not only that, but I like elephant-foot tables even less than I like purple walls. Yes, if a person were ever to have come up to me—taking a survey of likes and dislikes or some such thing—I should have most certainly told that person that above all things I dislike purple walls and elephant-foot tables. Unfortunately, I have arrived home, to the beloved place of my birth, the comfortable, unchanging haven I dreamed about all those years I was away, to find that I am the possessor of both a purple saloon and elephant-foot tables—three elephant-foot tables to be precise about the business. I have to tell you, Beck, it's damned depressing."

Beck, whose mouth had fallen open at Fletcher's first words, brushed past his employer, his straight left leg swinging out widely as he raced clumsily through the foyer to stand at the entranceway to the yellow saloon. His eyes nearly popped out of his head as he surveyed the scene before him. "My God," he said on a groan, his voice hushed with awe. "She said . . . But I never thought . . . I never imagined. She did it. The daft woman actually did it."

Now, this was interesting, or at least Fletcher thought so. "You must tell me more, my friend." Fletcher slid his arm around Beck's shoulders so that the two of them could stand and gaze in wonder at the changes Aunt Belleville had wrought. "I did hear you correctly, didn't I? You did know Aunt Belleville was considering just such a redecoration?"

Beck nodded, swallowing hard. "She did talk about it once or twice. Only in passing, you understand. She had seen just such an arrangement somewhere and thought it the height of fashion."

"And here I was, wondering if my dear aunt was feeling at home in my house. It seems I shouldn't have worried. The only question remaining is whether or not she will feel equally enamored with the height of fashion once it is installed in her bedchamber, for that is where those tables are going, you know. Will we have to get someone to carry them, do you suppose, or will they whistle to heel and follow us there?"

"But your aunt, Fletcher? How will she take this? She'll be crushed that you don't like it. Do you seriously believe you can redo the saloon without hurting her?"

"You're questioning my abililty to bring my aunt around to my way of thinking? Me? The man known far and wide for his soothing manner and velvet tongue? I'm aghast!" Fletcher raised his eyebrows challengingly. "I assume this question will be resolved with our usual wager?"

"Don't be so cocksure of yourself, Fletch," Beck warned. "Remember, I made a small fortune when Miss Denham opted to marry Vincent Mayhew."

A small tic began to work in Fletcher's cheek and Beck was instantly contrite. Although he knew the worst was over and Fletcher wished all that was wonderful for his friend, the Earl of Hawkhurst, the experience of not being able to win the woman he wanted was still too new for Beck to mention it to the man in a teasing way. "I'm sorry, Fletch."

"Sorry?" Fletcher responded as if shocked by his friend's apology. "What are you sorry about? If you're referring to Christine, you should know that I am not harboring a bruised heart over the incident. She and Vincent were born to be together. I consider myself fortunate that I had some small part in bringing them to the altar. However, if you are sorry about the elephant feet, I am more than willing to accept your apology—and your wager. Only, please, do something about the saloon before I am reduced to tears and stamping my feet. It wouldn't be a pretty sight, Beck, I am warning you now."

"I'll arrange for the saloon to be repainted immediately," Beck promised, knowing Fletcher was angrier than he was pretending to be. How could his friend's aunt have done such a thing? He had listened to her fanciful plans many times, but he had never seriously believed she would . . . "Good God, no! The music room."

Once more Beck was off, with Fletcher following along behind at a leisurely pace. Beck rounded a corner in the hallway, nearly colliding with Lethbridge, who looked down on him from his superior height and intoned deeply, "I beg your pardon," in that condescending way of his that always set Beck's teeth on edge, before stepping aside to let the younger man pass.

"Mr. Belden, I have ordered a cold collation delivered to the morning room as soon as possible," the butler continued, seeing his employer. "There will be a selection of local meats, breads, and fruits, of course, and I have taken the liberty of ordering a bottle up from the cellars by way of celebrating your safe return from the wars."

"You're too kind, Lethbridge. Always were," Fletcher told the man, looking past him to watch Beck disappear into the music room, already knowing that the room was the same as he, Fletcher, had left it five years earlier. "Tell me, Lethbridge, do you know what plans my aunt has for the music room?"

Lethbridge's chin lifted a fraction. "Suffice it to say, sir, that they were unfortunate, and best forgotten. We shall not be considering them."

"We shan't?" Fletcher repeated, his lips quivering at Lethbridge's proprietorial tone. It seemed everyone believed they had a right to decide what was best for Lakeview. Everyone but him, that was. Feeling vaguely out of sorts once more, he tipped his head to one side and said, "You know something, Lethbridge? I think I should like the cold collation you described so beautifully served on the porch outside the music room—if that meets with your approval, of course."

The butler's pockmarked face, which bore mute witness to the fact that the man had survived a long-ago case of smallpox, flushed a deep red. Bowing, he said, "I shall see to it at once, sir," and backed away, as if unable to trust himself to say more. He still managed to look more austere than servile, and made Fletcher feel as if he had just kicked a bear and had a lucky escape, thanks only to the generosity of the bear, who had graciously deigned not to eat him.

Beck joined him in the hallway, looking over his shoulder curiously at Lethbridge as the butler passed by him. Turning his attention to his employer, he asked, "What did you say to him, Fletch? The man looks slightly affronted, if I read his expression correctly. Can't I leave you alone for a moment without you doing some sort of damage with that twisted humor of yours? Is there anyone here that you haven't insulted?"

"Where do you want these things? Or are you going to just stand there, watching my back break?" came an aggrieved voice from the open doorway behind them. The two men turned to look at Billy, who was engaged in a Herculean contest with several heavy pieces of baggage, and apparently losing the struggle.

"Don't tell me," Beck said with a wave of one hand. "Let me guess. Could this be the cheeky groom? What did you say to set the lad against you?"

Fletcher shook his head as he watched the slim young lad trying to deal with the heavy baggage. The boy's arrogance, unaccented speech, and rude station in life were infinitely jarring to Fletcher's sense of order, and the scent of mystery he had sniffed at their first meeting returned with twice the force.

"Abominable little brat, isn't he? Why, Beck, I did a horrible thing, of course," Fletcher answered matter-of-factly. "Truly reprehensible. I asked him to come out into the rain to tend to my animals. Do you think a horsewhipping is good enough, or would you, Lethbridge, and most assuredly this young man like to make up a firing squad and have me shot at dawn?"

Beck went forward to assist the all-but-toppling groom, relieving him of the largest of the many pieces of baggage and heading for the staircase. "Follow me, young man," he said, directing a condemning glare at his employer. "If that is all right with you, Mr. Belden?"

Fletcher bowed to his friend. "I am entirely at your command, Beck," he said genially, "but it might be best if you asked young Master Smith here if it is agreeable to him, for opinions, usually unsolicited, seem to be his strongest suit. Master Smith?" he inquired, measuring the groom's reaction with his intelligent gray gaze.

Billy adjusted her grip on one of the remaining cases and shrugged. "Suits me to a cow's thumb," she said, her voice so gruff Fletcher was tempted to ask if it was possible the groom was sickening for something after a single dose of warm rainwater. "Lord knows there's enough out there for an army. What did you do—bring London with you?"

Fletcher watched in amused fascination as Beck's eyes widened to show white all around the clear-blue irises that had prompted his mother to name him after the local dialect for a brook. Clearly even the outspoken Beck had been struck by the blatant disrespect the groom was showing the master of the house.

"Not that I won't carry them all, and be thankful to do it," Billy hastened to add, looking from one man to the other apprehensively, as if just realizing that she had crossed the line—again.

"That's cursed good of you, Master Smith," Fletcher told him, turning away to hide the delight he felt. This boy could prove very interesting. Just what he needed to clear his mind of London and the memories of Arabella that had struck him so forcefully as he stepped inside Lakeview—as well as the faint but lingering pain of his recent, unrewarding brush with romance.

Beck, with a sinking feeling in the pit of his stomach, as he had long ago learned to recognize when his friend was about to engage in a lark, waited for what was to come next.

He didn't have long to wait.

"Beck," Fletcher said, turning to saunter to the staircase, "once luncheon is over, would you please be so kind as to pack a few changes of clothes for me—nothing fancy, you understand. I do believe I should like to set out tomorrow at first light for an inspection of my land and a short tour of the Lake District itself. Not above a week, I should say. I've missed the lapwings, but there is still much to see. Pack no more than will fit comfortably behind a saddle."

Knowing he was only asking the question his friend wished him to ask, Beck put forth fatalistically, "But you know I can't ride along with you, Fletch, thanks to this cursed leg. Are you planning to go alone?"

"Alone, dear man? Good God, no. Who should pull off my boots if I were to go alone? Who should make up my bed beneath the stars if I don't wish to sleep at some inferior inn? No, Beck, I shall take young Smith with me. Surely you knew that?"

"Me?" Billy exploded, dropping the case she had just succeeded in tucking beneath her arm. "You want me? Of all the cork-headed ideas I've ev—" Her voice halted abruptly and she clamped a hand to her mouth, aghast.

"You see, Beck?" Fletcher remarked silkily. "The lad is overjoyed—and belatedly lost for words. He shall make an admirable companion," he said, turning to look levelly at Billy, "and we shall be able to get to know each other much, much better. Won't we, Master Smith?''

Billy hung her head. ''I imagine so, sir,'' she whispered wretchedly, then brightened. ''But I don't ride, sir.''

Fletcher made a great business out of adjusting his lace shirt cuffs. ''Then I suggest you learn, Master Smith. Leave the baggage where you've so conveniently dropped it and go posthaste to direct Hedge to give you a lesson this afternoon. Shall we both say a prayer that he is sober? I shouldn't wish for you to show up outside tomorrow morning sitting backward on a pony.''

''Fletch, don't you think—''

''No, Beck,'' Fletcher cut off his friend, sending a silent warning with his eyes. ''I don't think; I know. I have a great need for a communion with nature only a few days spent riding the district on horseback can provide me. I have a vague notion of ridding my mind of the dissipations of town life, and as you cannot accompany me and as Hedge is out of the question, Billy here will do quite nicely.'' He raised one eyebrow and looked down on the groom. ''Are you still here? Shouldn't your time be better spent learning how to ride? And cheer up. We shall have a splendid time, I'm convinced of it.''

''I know how to ride,'' Billy muttered angrily. ''Who'd hire a groom that couldn't ride?''

''Who, indeed?'' Fletcher answered, grateful the young lad wasn't armed, or he'd be a dead man for sure. ''It would be absurd, wouldn't it? But I applaud your attack of honesty. What, ho?'' He stepped past the groom to peer through the open doorway to the drive. ''Speaking of absurdities, Beck, it would appear my aunt has returned to the bosom of her family and is now all aflutter to discover that I have arrived home in her absence. Bring that case back down here and leave it, please, my friend. I shouldn't wish to greet the dear woman alone."

Billy, with a grudging tug on her forelock that would have made Lethbridge's starchy demeanor appear to be blatant toad-eating, made good her escape, leaving the case she had been carrying directly in the middle of the hallway, and directly in Fletcher's path.

Fletcher watched Billy go, mentally toting up the groom's size and subtracted another year from the age he'd believed his groom to be, before pushing the case to the side with one booted toe and holding out his arms to his aunt.

The woman, who was in the process of running full-tilt up the broad steps, calling her nephew's name—her short stature and considerable girth combining with her penchant for filmy, flowing draperies immediately putting Fletcher in mind of an ungainly fishing boat in full sail—accidentally gifted Billy with a glancing blow, sending the slighter body careening into one thick round white post of the portico. Instantly contrite, Aunt Belleville turned back to minister to her victim, grabbing at the groom's upper arm just as that abused person made to rise, causing Billy to topple completely to the ground.

"Oh, dear, oh, dear, are you all right, child?" Aunt Belleville inquired with deep concern, for she was always neck-high with deep concern for something or someone. "Here," she said kindly, stepping directly and with her full weight onto Billy's hand, "let me help you up."

"He might manage it fairly well on his own, Aunt," Fletcher suggested dryly, standing behind her, "once you remove your foot from his paw, of course."

Aunt Belleville jumped back at once, exclaiming, "Oh, my! Did I do that? How could I have done that? I might have crippled the poor lamb for life. I only meant to help."

Fletcher gently took hold of the old woman's arm, watching as Billy got to her feet, rubbed at her hand, and took off for the safety of the stables, muttering under her breath. "Of course you did, Aunt. You haven't an unkind bone in your body, and we all will swear to it, won't we, Beck? Tell me, my dearest, these poor sick people you have been visiting. Neither of them is dead now, I trust."

"Fletch," Beck warned quietly, doing his best not to laugh as the three of them walked into the foyer just as Lethbridge, who had obviously heard the commotion and come to check on his ladylove, directed a housemaid to begin carrying the baggage to the master's room.

Aunt Belleville was immediately diverted. "Your chamber, Fletcher," she exclaimed, clutching his arm so tightly it put him in fear for the survival of his new jacket. "Oh, my goodness! Oh, my goodness, my goodness. But I didn't know. How could I know? I couldn't, could I? You never wrote, never let me know. It was only when I saw the coach that I knew—that I dared hope—and here you are, with us all at sixes and sevens. Yet what was I to do, what with Henry Dillworth breaking his foot in that fall and his wife just getting over her bilious attack and all but begging me to help her? But that is no excuse, is it, for family must always come first, and well I know it. I should have anticipated, that's what I should have done. What a poor opinion you must have of me! Please forgive me, Fletcher, and brace yourself."

"Brace myself, Aunt?" Fletcher echoed, aiding the woman as she divested herself of her half-dozen shawls in fear she might yet contrive to smother herself with one of them. "You have bad news for me?"

Aunt Belleville bit her lip, then plunged ahead, revealing dramatically, "Indeed I do, dearest. Your chamber is not ready for you."

"If that means you have not redecorated it, Aunt, let me assure you that I shall strive to bear up under the disappointment," Fletcher told her, willing himself not to wince as they entered the yellow saloon and the violent purple assaulted his senses.

There were times—not many of them, granted—but times Aunt Belleville could be perceptive. This was one of them. She subsided into a chair and looked around the room. "You don't like it, do you, Fletcher?" She gave a heartfelt sigh. "I had so hoped—"

"I'm a cad. A thoughtless, thankless cad," Fletcher intoned sorrowfully, shaking his head as Beck sat down on a nearby settee, pulling a face at his friend's execrable acting. "But I must admit it, Aunt, breathtaking as it is, I cannot like it. You see, I had kept a picture of this room in my heart while I was away, and I believe I need to see this fond picture brought to life once more now that I am home." He shook his head and sat down beside Beck. "I should have been more thoughtful. I should have perished, my dream intact, and not burdened you with my ungrateful reaction to your splendid good taste."

"Then you do like it!" Aunt Belleville exclaimed,

clapping her hands as her conformable mind too in only what it wished to hear. "I knew you would. But I understand how you are feeling, my boy. I once had a gown, a lovely pink satin with little bits of lace tacked all along the scalloped hem, that I tried to duplicate in green, everything the same down to the last scallop." She shrugged, eloquently spreading her hands. "It wasn't the same, of course. It was the pink or nothing."

"I'm so pleased that you understand, Aunt," Fletcher said, grinning triumphantly at Beck, who, mentally kicking himself for allowing Fletcher's single failure make him believe the man had lost his unerring touch in dealing with females, reached into his pocket to withdraw a guinea and place it in Fletcher's outstretched hand. "Thank you, Beck," he said quietly, slipping the coin into his own pocket. "I shan't so insult you as to bite on it first to see if it is genuine."

Aunt Belleville, who had been in the midst of fanning herself with a lace handkerchief and therefore thankfully hadn't noticed this last exchange, sat forward to stare at her nephew. "Fletcher," she began in a quavering voice, "why are you home? There is a most wonderful party going on in London. I know that because, even way up here, away from everything, we have heard about it. The princes and princesses, the parties, the fêtes . . . Are you ill?" She wiggled herself forward even farther, to sit perched on the very end of the chair. "Of course you are ill! Oh, dear, all that festivity, all the rich food, and too much drink as well, I should suppose. You're burnt to the socket. Yes, I see it now. You have a certain drained look to you, hasn't he, Beck? See it"—her own eyes narrowed as she pointed to Fletcher—"right there, around the eyes?"

Beck, who knew it was time and more that he got a little of his own back, leaned across the settee to peer into his employer's eyes. "Yes, yes, Miss Belleville, you're right. I see it too." He turned to look at the woman. "What do you think? A good dose of salts might do the trick." He turned back to Fletcher, his face a study in concerned condemnation. "And you wanted to go haring about the countryside, sleeping outside and eating as catch can. Shame on you, Fletch."

3

It hadn't been easy, but Fletcher had finally convinced his aunt that, contrary to what he privately believed to be the woman's fondest hope, he was not in fact sickening for something and in need of her ministrations. Even more difficult to bring home to the woman was his reasoning for abandoning her at first light to go traveling through the Lake District on horseback with naught but a groom to accompany him.

In the first place, she declared, ever since overseas travel had suffered such a dreary setback during the war, the district had been inundated with flighty young men taking walking tours and otherwise using the excuse of sightseeing for all sorts of rumpus-making in the area. As a result, anything even vaguely interesting left to see, Aunt Belleville reasoned, would be overrun with young dandies on a spree, and Fletcher wouldn't like that above half, now, would he?

And in the second place, Aunt Belleville had declared rationally, hadn't her dear nephew just driven through a good part of the district in order to arrive at Lakeview, which was in nearly the exact center of the area? How many hills and cows and sheep did one man need to see before he could feel satisfied he had seen enough, for goodness' sake? The whole idea did not make sense to the woman.

Beck, of course, had been less than no help at all, taking Aunt Belleville's side with a joyful perverseness that had left Fletcher longing to land him a facer. He had pointed out that the owner of Lakeview should perhaps begin his touring a little closer to home, checking up on matters concerning the estate itself. Fletcher had looked askance at his friend, knowing the jolly little devil would have to be "rewarded" for his disloyalty.

But in the end Fletcher had won out, and his aunt, who had, after calmly handing her nephew the Bible, reminding him it was his duty to lead them all in their evening prayers, finally retired to her chamber, to decide where best to place the three elephant-foot tables Fletcher had warned her were going to take up residence with her the following day.

Fletcher had just finished a huge breakfast and was heading for the front door, still chuckling over the lengthy list of chores he had left behind for Beck—with the repainting of the saloon topping the list—when Lethbridge crossed his path, a large black umbrella in his hand.

"It will be dampening down before long," the butler pronounced heavily, employing the local, optimistic expression for what was sure to be a downpour bordering on a deluge, "and your aunt expressly wished for you to take this with you."

Looking at the huge contraption and mentally picturing himself on horseback with the thing opened above his head, Fletcher thanked the butler but demurred. "But only think, Lethbridge, I'd have no one to refold the dammed thing," he pointed out kindly. "I'd be forced to leave it in a ditch. Please convey my thanks, and my regrets, to my aunt."

The butler held the umbrella out once more, just like a tollgate-keeper refusing to raise his gate, showing a marked reluctance to allow his master to pass. "She was most adamant, sir," he pursued severely.

Fletcher shook his head in wry amusement. "Ah, Lethbridge, you've got it bad, don't you? Very well. If you promise not to compromise my dear aunt while I am gone, I shall take the umbrella." He'd take it as far as the stable, Fletcher told himself silently, although he saw no reason to impart this last piece of information to the lovestruck butler.

Lethbridge overlooked the insult to concentrate on the positive: he had achieved his objective, which would ease dear Miss Belleville's worried heart. "Very good, sir. I knew you would see the rightness of the thing." The butler quickly handed over the large umbrella and stepped smartly forward to open the front door. "We shall look forward to seeing you within the week, sir. Have a most pleasant journey, sir. And have I told you, sir, how happy the entire staff is to have you safely home with us once more?"

"Don't grovel, Lethbridge," Fletcher warned genially. "It doesn't become you, and makes me damned uneasy into the bargain. Oh, and Lethbridge," he added, turning back just as he had been about to walk onto the porch, "why don't you take some time for yourself when I get back? Don't you have a cousin in Bath worth visiting? Beck tells me you haven't been away from Lakeview since I left for the Peninsula. You deserve a change of scene, a look at some of the rest of the world. I'm sure we can muddle through without you for at least a fortnight."

"And why should I do that, sir?"

"You are looking sheep's eyes at my aunt and you

can ask that question?'' Fletcher shook his head. ''Perhaps it's already too late. Ah, well, just don't make me have to get out my late father's blunderbuss, will you, Lethbridge?''

The butler, coloring to the roots of his receding hairline, closed the front door without another word, leaving a chuckling Fletcher outside on the portico as the weather, which had been gray since dawn, turned suddenly wet.

Fletcher's smile faded as he realized that he was quite alone. There was no Pagan, his favorite mount, his saddle packed and ready for adventure, waiting for him. There was no second horse, similarly laden, to serve as mount for his cheeky young groom. But—and this was most damning of all—there was no Billy Smith to be seen anywhere.

His gray eyes narrowed, Fletcher set out for the stable, his boot heels striking sharply against the gravel path as his many-caped drab coat billowed out behind him and raindrops gathered into a puddle inside the curved brim of his hat.

Fletcher threw open the door to the stable so that it crashed against the wall, startling the horses into whinnying and pulling against their halter ropes in their stalls, and stepped inside, to stand very still for a moment as his eyes became accustomed to the dimness. He saw his personal saddle perched atop a low wall, his rolled baggage beside it, and his jaw set.

Pagan, the huge black in the first stall, recognized his master and moved to hang his head over the front of the half-door as Fletcher approached, searching in his pocket for a carrot he had commandeered from the kitchens.

"Presently, Pagan, presently," Fletcher told the stallion, which showed all the signs of being ready for a good run. "First I do believe I shall have to fight a battle of wills with a recalcitrant young groom—if I can locate him, that is. I can only hope he hasn't already loped off somewhere, knowing I've seen through his disguise. I didn't used to be so unsubtle. I must be getting old, Pagan, which is a lowering thought indeed, and yet another grievance I shall hold over Master Smith's head, as I wouldn't have entertained the notion of age at all if it hadn't been for him."

Leaving the horse for the moment, Fletcher walked along the long row of stalls that lined either side of the stable, looking into each stall in the hope of discovering his truant groom. Pausing in front of the last stall, he at last located his quarry, curled up in a corner of the small enclosed area, fast asleep atop a mound of fresh straw.

He unlatched the half-door quietly and entered the stall, walking up to Billy to deliver a short, sharp poke to the groom's hindquarters with the tip of the umbrella. "Come on, slugabed, time to get up!"

There was an immediate, very vocal response as a small hand snaked out to push the umbrella to one side. "Ow! Hey, what do you think you're doing, you sapskull? Can't ye see I'm sleeping? Who do you think you're poking anyway, Hedge? I've got a good mind to . . . Oh, Lord!"

"Oh, Lord, indeed, Master Smith," Fletcher repeated with as much *hauteur* as he could muster, dropping the umbrella and deliberately putting his fists on his hips and trying to look intimidating, a feat that was, according to Beck, impossible to achieve, thanks to his youthful blond good looks and perpetually laughing eyes. "I thought I had made it clear that we had planned to be on our way at first light?"

Billy scrambled to her feet, a thundercloud aspect on her small face, and growled, "We didn't plan anything. It was all your idea, and a worse one I cannot remember since your aunt thought it would be a jolly good idea to paint the stables pink. Can't you hear? It's raining fit to flood out there."

"And the sun will be shining before noon, if it isn't already shining on the other side of the hill. You know that, Master Smith, as well as I do. Besides, you look as if you could do with a good bath. Do you really sleep in here every night? Why don't you sleep in with Hedge? Surely there's more than one cot in the room. I am not so niggardly an employer as to have my people bedding down in stalls."

Billy rolled her eyes at this last bit of nonsense, willing to overlook his insult concerning her personal cleanliness because he was right: bathing head to foot with any frequency at Lakeview was a problem she had yet to overcome. "You don't know much, do you?" she retorted, too sleepy and out of sorts to guard her tongue. "No one in their right mind ever stands, yet alone sleeps, downwind of Hedge. He hasn't seen soap or water in twenty years."

"Thirty would have been my guess," Fletcher replied, grinning. "Now let's be on with it. I want to reach Langdale before dinner, with time to take in my surroundings at my leisure along the way."

Billy pushed out her lower lip. "I haven't even broken my fast." She was very hungry, having only picked at her evening meal before spending a decidedly unquiet night in dread of what morning would bring. Yet she knew better than to mention that she also hadn't had any time alone to take care of her bodily functions or make use of her toothpowder, which was one of the few things she had brought with her upon leaving home some two months earlier.

"Don't pucker up at me, Master Smith," Fletcher warned, turning away before the highly amusing sight of Billy, the indignant young groom's dark curls stuck with straw, goaded him into unleashing a shout of laughter. He saw a small bundle of carefully folded clothing sitting in a small wooden box, and bent to pick it up. Flinging it in the general direction of the groom, he ordered, "Find something to wrap this in, and let's get on with it. I'll saddle Pagan myself. Which mount is yours?"

He heard a slight shuffling behind him as Billy sat down to begin struggling into her boots. "The chestnut," she admitted, her tone giving evidence to her disgust.

"Buttercup?" Fletcher exclaimed, turning about just as Billy was shrugging into a three-sizes-too-large jacket. "A lovely mare, I'm sure, but she's nearly as old as I am."

Billy sniffed her agreement. "Probably older. Hedge says I'm to ride Buttercup or nothing. But you're right, sir. I wouldn't be able to keep up with you if I rode Buttercup, and you wouldn't like that. It will be a terrible disappointment, sir, but I am probably needed here anyway," she added sorrowfully, "what with all the horseflesh you brought with you and Hedge complaining about his rheumatism. He asked me what he might do for it."

"Why do I know, do you suppose, that you had a solution handy to offer to him?"

Billy grinned in spite of herself, for once feeling in charity with her employer. "You're right. I told Hedge to try a clean shirt."

Fletcher's lips twitched appreciatively at Billy's wit. "An admirable suggestion." He stepped outside the stall before turning to face his groom. "And how noble you are, Master Smith, and self-sacrificing as well, to be thinking of my comfort. I swear, your unselfishness fair bids to unman me. If nothing else, it makes me want to gift you with something that is worthy of your devotion. I know," he said, snapping his fingers. "I shall reward you by allowing you to ride She-Devil, the other horse I brought with me from London."

Fletcher saw the groom's green eyes brighten with sudden anticipation and delight, only to narrow assessingly and shift warily away from his gaze. "She-Devil, sir? Are you sure?"

"Oh, of course. How silly of me," Fletcher said, sighing. "I should have realized. She-Devil's far too much horse for a small lad like you."

"Too much horse? Too much horse! I can ride as well as you—better than you," Billy exclaimed, her hands bunching into fists as she readied to do battle with this odious, condescending man. She had sat her first pony before she could walk, and had been riding anything with four legs and a mane ever since. Who did Fletcher Belden think he was to stand there, grinning like an ape, and tell her she couldn't ride that sweet-going filly he had probably paid a small fortune for at Tatt's? Did he think she'd jump her over a cliff or some such foolishness?

"That remains to be seen," Master Smith," Fletcher pointed out dryly, moving toward Pagan's stall. "Perhaps I shall give you a chance to prove your horsemanship once we are on the road. That is, if you think you can be ready in ten minutes, for I am leaving then, with you or without you, as I am beginning to believe you are more trouble than you are worth."

Billy stood stock-still, biting her full bottom lip. This was her chance. He was giving her a way out, if she chose to take it. If she chose to take it? What was she thinking of? Of course she would take it; she would grab at it with both hands. Hadn't she spent nearly the entire night worrying and wondering how she could possibly conceal her identity if the two of them were to spend every minute together for the next several days?

She reached up to brush her fingers through her hair, angrily yanking at the bits of straw that clung to her curls. She'd need to cut her hair again soon or give the game away, she thought randomly. The game! Why on earth had she referred to what she was doing as a game? It was a lot of things, but a game it most certainly was not. This was serious. This was life-and-death, for pity's sake!

And now she had an opportunity—and a golden opportunity at that—to learn all about the real Fletcher Belden. After all, she was not about to have escaped from the pot only to launch herself headfirst into the fire.

Besides, he had challenged her. Her eyelids narrowed as she weighed the chance of being unmasked against the thrill of showing Fletcher Belden up in a race across country. She had already exercised She-Devil for a short while the previous afternoon, and knew the mare to have strong legs and a good heart. With a reasonable head start—and with a smidgeon of manufactured luck—she just might be able to beat Fletcher Belden, in more ways than one.

Giving herself no more to think, a devilish smile lighting her freckled face, Billy slammed a worn brown hat down over her ears, gathered up her small store of clothing, and headed for She-Devil's stall.

They were in a clean-smelling grassy meadow beneath an old thorn tree, its lower trunk wearing a blanket of wool left behind by the sheep that rubbed against it. The remnants of the meal Fletcher had solicited at a nearby inn were spread in front of them on the blanket Billy had unearthed from her tied bundle. Their horses were tied up to branches and munching on some tender new leaves on a nearby bush.

It was a lovely spot, surrounded by green hills dotted with wildflowers, with the snow-topped Langdale Pikes behind them. From somewhere high in the tree a black-and-white pied wagtail called to its mate in a constantly repeated chirp that sounded, to Billy, as if the bird was saying "tee-up, tee-up." In the distance, a small flock of sheep was being guarded by a vigilant border collie, and the only note of melancholy in the entire scene was the constant lowing of dairy cows for the calves that had been taken from them shortly after birth for the good of the milk.

The morning, which had gotten off to such a shaky if not sodden start, had improved considerably once they were on their way. The sun had come out to dry the land and lift the smell of wildflowers into the air.

Billy, her stomach full and her body comfortably lazy, lay on her side, her head propped on one hand, staring at a busy honeybee that was buzzing from flower to flower gathering pollen. She was feeling more in charity with Fletcher Belden than she had since their first meeting.

He was, all things considered, she had decided, a fairly likable if frippery fellow, for he was lying on his side on the other edge of the blanket at that moment, wearing a self-made daisy chain around his blond head and a self-satisfied grin on his handsome face. He was also a good traveling companion, if her small experience of one half-day spent riding alongside him was to be any indication of the tone that would prevail for the remainder of their time together.

They had ridden across country whenever possible, Fletcher speaking nostalgically and humorously about his rake-helly youth spent in these hills and valleys, which Billy considered to be the most beautiful in England. He had told her of some of his youthful exploits with Beck before that man had injured his leg, recounting carefree days spent bird-nesting, rowing, hunting for wood pigeons and rabbits, rock-climbing, fishing—even skating in the winter time.

It sounded idyllic and much like her own childhood, a childhood that had been radically altered five years previously, before being totally destroyed three months ago. Billy shook her head, purposely banishing her unhappy thoughts, and did her best to concentrate once more on the buzzing bee.

''Billy?'' Her head jerked upward, her attention caught by Fletcher's voice. Hastening to get to her knees, she bent to gather up the scraps on the blanket, only to stop abruptly as he continued, ''Do you think we can cry friends?''

Averting her eyes, Billy shrugged, answering, "I don't know if that is proper, sir. After all, you are the master and I am but a lowly groom."

Fletcher tugged at the whimsical daisy chain, dislodging it so that it hung down over one eye. "If you are a groom, Master Smith, I am Old Swellfoot."

Recognizing the hint of sarcasm in his voice, Billy continued her housekeeping efforts with a vengeance, hoping her lack of an answer would put an end to the discussion.

This, of course, was a vain hope, as Beck or Vincent Mayhew or any of Fletcher's various acquaintances could have told her. "Forgive me for pestering you when you obviously don't wish to discuss it, but I sense a certain want of openness in our association that I wish to breach. I'll try to say this as kindly as possible—and please remember that my questions are without malice and are concerned with your well-being rather than simple curiosity."

"Yes, sir," Billy grumbled, inwardly steeling herself for what was to come next.

"Thank you for your kind indulgence. Now, tell me, was it very terrible at home, Master Smith?" Fletcher pursued doggedly, the daisy chain now dangling from his left forefinger. "Perhaps your Latin master caned you—or was it perhaps the advent of a wicked stepmother that set you out on the road?"

Billy considered these options, weighing them silently in her head as possible explanations, for obviously she was going to have to offer Fletcher some reason for her appearance at Lakeview. She'd have to be careful, for it was obvious that Belden wasn't a stupid man—not that it would have taken anyone with a halfpenny's more intelligence than the drunken Hedge to see through her thin disguise, and well she knew it. But wait. Fletcher had only seen through part of her disguise. He still believed himself to be dealing with a runaway boy.

A small smile tickled the corners of Billy's mouth for a moment before she brought her ill-timed humor under control. He wanted a story, did he, this maddeningly inquisitive man? Well, then, a story was just what he would get.

"It—it's my brother, sir," she improvised wildly, the corners of her mouth now deliberately drooping. "We're orphans, you understand, with our father dying last summer. George is off at Oxford taking orders, leaving me behind with a paid companion we cannot afford. I—I decided it would be better for George if I struck out on my own, to make a decent wage, until he can support us—"

"Is that right?" Fletcher interrupted. "It's a good thing Aunt Belleville isn't here, for your story would surely tug most painfully at her tender heartstrings."

Caught up in her lie, she added bravely, "Yes, sir. I even send George some money when I can, for I love him that dearly. George is so happy now, and his last letter—the one I received a few months ago—told me that he has met a wonderful young lady, the daughter of a local shopkeeper, and very genteel. They shall probably marry, which would be above all things wonderful, because then I should be able to live with them until George gets a position. But, until then, I knew that I had to do something to help George—for he is the best of brothers—so I ran away. That's all there is to it," she ended, proud of herself, and popped a crust of bread into her mouth.

Fletcher hadn't moved more than one expressive eyebrow throughout the entire dissertation, his gray eyes continuing to search her green ones as if to gauge the veracity of the story. "George is a very lucky man. Very fortunate, indeed. I'm proud of you, Master Smith, for your unselfish love and devotion. You even send him money?"

"Yes, sir," Billy answered carefully, knowing she was blushing and hoping her pink cheeks would strike Fletcher as being the result of her modesty and his praise rather than the flush of guilt. She took another bite of crust, deliberately filling her mouth so that she wouldn't give herself away by saying too much. She may have already gone too far with the bit about sending the fictitious George money.

"Tell me, what's her name?" Fletcher questioned silkily, the daisy chain now rotating around his lazily swinging finger, so that Billy inhaled sharply, nearly choking on the bread.

"Her—her name?" she gulped out between betraying coughs. "Whose name?"

"George's fiancée, of course, Master Smith," Fletcher pursued, causing Billy to wish there was another crust of bread so that she could stuff it down his grinning throat. He knew, curse him! He had done it again—found her out—and with the same elementary tactic.

It wouldn't be any great feat for her to come up with a name; heaven knew she had been accused more than once of having the devil's own affinity for manufactured truths, but she was also no fool. The story—a spur-of-the-moment affair—had been offered and summarily rejected. She would fall back and advance on another front.

The tears brought on by her fit of coughing standing

her in good stead, she squeezed her eyes shut tightly and willed herself to produce a few more. "I—I'm so sorry, Mr. Belden. There is no woman," she admitted quietly, adding a short sob for good measure as she sniffed and swiped at her eyes with the back of her hand.

"How you amaze me, Master Smith. Tell me—is there a George, or is the so lucky brother also nonexistent?"

Throwing herself face front on the blanket just as she hoped any thwarted young boy would, Billy shook her head in answer to the question while she cudgeled her brains for inspiration; then she sat back on her haunches, pulled a large red handkerchief from her breeches pocket, and noisily blew her nose.

"There's no George, or at least not for me," she said brokenly. "He ran away to sea when our father died, saying he wanted to kill Boney. He really wanted to get away from our father's creditors, who came and took everything—even my favorite top, which could be of no good to anyone but me, could it? It was red and green and I truly loved it. I was supposed to go to some dead-old distant aunt—in Tunbridge Wells of all places! I—I couldn't do it, so I ran away. You won't send me back, Mr. Belden, sir, will you? She'll make me eat gruel and—and read sermons!"

"She sounds like an ugly customer, although most dead-old distant aunts are not known for their *joie de vivre*. And I agree. Sermons can be murderously off-putting," Fletcher said, his tone commiserating, "as can evening prayers, come to think of it. But, Smith, your aunt must be worried to death, wondering what has become of you. You're much too young, halfling, to be out on your own."

Now Billy became belligerent, for she believed it was time she showed some hint of spunk. Sticking out her small chin, she retorted, "I'm ten-and-three, sir—no sniveling infant. There's many a fellow my age who has already been out on his own for years."

Fletcher pushed himself up to a sitting position, a move Billy countered by standing up, for she had found she liked it better when she was looking down on him rather than straight into his eyes. "I suggest we leave further discussion of the right and wrong of the road you have chosen for later this evening when we are settled at an inn, although I must tell you I applaud your candor in telling me the truth, even if I did have to listen to that whopping crammer about George and his ladylove before you decided to make a clean breast of things."

"Thank you, sir," Billy mumbled humbly, feeling rather proud of herself.

"However," Fletcher added warningly, rising so that he, whether he knew it or not, had the upper hand on her once more, "I would very much appreciate it if you would tell me your real name. Master Smith is much too ordinary an appellation for a quick-witted fellow like yourself."

Billy bent to retrieve the blanket, shaking it free of crumbs and refolding it carefully so that it would fit behind her saddle. She had done it! He had actually believed her! She could afford to be magnanimous. Holding the folded blanket against her breast, she sniffed once more, for effect, and said quietly, "It's Belchem. William Belchem. My father was a teacher near Keswick."

"Keswick," Fletcher repeated conversationally,

heading for his mount. "Lovely place. Near Ullswater, isn't it?"

"Keswick is several miles from Ullswater. You mean Derwent Water, don't you, sir? But then there are so many lakes, aren't there?" Billy corrected politely, although she longed to box his ears. It was depressing to think that Fletcher could be so obvious, as she had begun to hope for better from him. Really, did he think he would be able to catch her out so easily?

"Do I? Oh, yes, of course I do," Fletcher said reflectively, mounting Pagan, who danced about, eager to be on the move once more. "I have been away too long. Silly mistake. My apologies, Master Belchem. Are you ready to ride?"

Billy bent to retrieve her hat, slamming it down over her ears as she approached She-Devil, not at all mollified by his apology for having doubted her. If he wasn't going to show a little more curiosity, keep her on her toes, as it were, this could prove to be a depressingly boring excursion. "I'm always ready to ride, Mr. Belden."

They cantered into the dusty yard of the Stag's Head in Bowness-on-Windemere while it was still light, Fletcher ordering Billy to leave the horses in the care of an ostler so that the groom could accompany him into the coffee room.

Billy's gaze moved apprehensively about the foul-smelling, low-ceilinged room. It was heavily populated with loud, boisterous men who would have laughed had anyone addressed them as gentlemen. She asked Fletcher, "Aren't you going to ask for a private dining parlor, sir?"

Fletcher looked down at his groom in amusement as he stripped off his riding gloves, for he had been noticing all day the odd squeamishness Billy seemed to exhibit at the silliest things. Take the stop they had made among a stand of trees when Fletcher had felt nature's call, for instance. Billy had all but run into the privacy of the woods to relieve himself, his temper flaring hotly when Fletcher had accused him of being missish.

"If you have something I haven't seen anywhere in my travels from here to the Peninsula and beyond," Fletcher had teased, "I should feel sorely deprived if you won't share a peek with me," earning himself a darkling look and, he was sure, a muffled curse, for his pains.

"You have something against downing your mutton in the company of strangers, hafling?" Fletcher asked now, seeing the innkeeper approaching. "Damned stuffy for a snotty-nosed runaway adventurer, ain't you?"

"It's not that," Billy told him peevishly. "It's just that I never before ate in a private parlor, and I should like to see one. And my nose isn't snotty," she added in an undertone. "It only runs when I cry."

"It does? How silly of me not to notice. I stand corrected," Fletcher said quietly before turning his attention to the innkeeper, who, having completed his mental totting up of Fletcher's person and deciding his latest customer was one of the quality, was busily bowing and scraping and touting the magnificence of his best private parlor and bedchamber.

Ten minutes later Fletcher and Billy were ensconced in a private dining room, for if the truth be told Fletcher hadn't really relished the idea of sitting elbow to elbow with a gaggle of strangers, whether it be to make polite conversation or watch in awe the magnitude of their ineptitude in the handling of simple eating utensils. He'd had enough of both during the celebrations in London. The plank table in front of them was piled high with cold meats, two whole chickens, and a variety of fruit, and the array of local foodstuffs warmed his heart.

"Make the most of it," Fletcher said, pulling off a chicken leg for himself, "for tomorrow night we will be sleeping beneath the stars."

Billy, who had been in the act of securing the other drumstick for herself, sat back, Fletcher's words effectively destroying what had until that moment been a raging hunger in her belly. "Why would you want to do that?" she asked, aghast. She had known he had spoken of doing just such a harebrained thing, but she hadn't really brought herself to believe it.

After all, what sensibly minded person would give up clean sheets and a roof over his head to sleep in a damp field surrounded by smelly sheep and all sorts of creeping things, and with the chance of rain pelting them at any moment? It was ludicrous, that's what it was. Besides, after two months of bedding down in the Lakeview stable, Billy had been looking forward to stretching out in a real bed.

"I do some of my best thinking out of doors," Fletcher responded, "not that I owe you an explanation. What, ho! My, my, and what have we here? Hello there, sweetings. Aren't you a pleasant surprise!"

Billy looked toward the doorway to see a barmaid coming into the room carrying two mugs of ale. Actually, Billy thought nastily, she saw what Fletcher must have seen, which was the barmaid's absolutely magnificent bosom.

The barmaid plunked down the two mugs, nearly knocking Billy off the plank seat with a swing of her full hips as she turned to Fletcher, to smile and wink, saying, "Will there be anythin' else yer'll be needin', sir? My name is Beatrice, sir, an' I'd be ever so pleased ter serve yer."

"Isn't that wonderful, Billy?" Fletcher asked, never removing his gaze from Beatrice's mind-boggling cleavage. He'd sworn off women for a while, but that did not mean he had been so foolish as to believe he could forsake fun. "And when would you be free to, um, serve me, Beatrice?"

Beatrice gave a toss of her dirty blond head. "Those louts in the coffee room will be home with their naggin' wives come midnight. Perhaps yer might loik a bit o'company then, sir? I kin be very, very good company."

"Oh, if that isn't above everything wonderful," Billy exclaimed, taking a deep drink of ale, which was her first experience with anything stronger than goat's milk. The liquid tasted vile, but she conquered the urge to spit it out. "And what am I supposed to be doing while the two of you cavort all over the place—hiding in the cupboard with my hands clapped over my ears?"

Fletcher slowly turned his head to skewer Billy with his iron-gray gaze. "As I recall, Billy, you spent last night tucked up in one of my stalls. May I suggest you go make friends with the ostler so that he might be so kind as to provide you with clean straw? Or, if you are not too fastidious or too wet behind the ears, perhaps dearest Beatrice here has a friend for you."

Billy's mouth opened and closed several times before

she stood, reached out to rip the remaining drumstick from the chicken, exclaimed, "I ain't in the petticoat line," and stomped out of the parlor, slamming the door behind her.

She stood in the narrow hallway for five minutes—or five years—trying her best to convince herself she didn't give a tinker's dam about what was or was not going on behind that closed door. It was no use—and it wasn't because she wanted the fool man for herself, because that was the farthermost thing from her mind. Wasn't it?

Put her out with the horses, would he, while he rutted like a stallion in heat? Well, she'd see about that. He was the one who belonged in the stables—him and his overripe mare. A parade of images, the next more perverse and upsetting than the last, invaded Billy's highly imaginative mind, her blind rage turning quickly to a deep, revenge-seeking anger.

Dredging up every ribald story Hedge had ever told her, and seeking to remember every indiscreet word ever spoken in her hearing over the years by any of the family servants, she scraped together the semblance of a plan.

The door to the private dining room opened at last and Beatrice came out, her smile, to Billy's mind, nearly as wide as her broad hips, her hands busily retying the strings of her blouse. Her flashing green eyes narrowed with rage, Billy stuck out her arm—still holding the greasy chicken leg in her hand—to block Beatrice's passage.

"Hold it right there, slut," she gritted out in her deepest possible voice, hoping she had remembered all the right words. "I don't know what you're planning, but hear this: that man is mine! He may trifle with you, only for a bit of slap and tickle, but it's me he sleeps with, and I don't want any filthy blowen like you giving him a dose of the pox."

The barmaid's mouth dropped to half-mast as her eyes widened to the size of saucers. She looked over her shoulder at the closed door, then back at Billy, running her gaze up and down the groom's thin body. "But he . . . But you're a . . . But we were goin' ter . . . Oh, no I won't! That's sick, that's what that is. I heard 'bout such queer goins-on, an' I'll have no part of it, does yer hear me? Yer kin have him. I doesn't want no man-milliner."

Billy dropped her arm to allow Beatrice to scamper past her, a small smile on her face as she realized she had achieved her objective. The innkeeper would be lucky if his barmaid stopped running before she reached Crook Common.

Her smile faded slightly, though, as she realized two more things.

First, she had no idea what she had said that had so frightened Beatrice. Had it bothered her so much that a small, flat-chested girl—for surely her disguise, which had so far deceived Fletcher, could not have fooled another woman—had dared to fight her for Fletcher? It made no sense.

And second, and much more damning now that she had rid herself of Beatrice, she had fated herself to sharing a bedchamber with Fletcher.

4

Fletcher and Billy climbed the stairs to the bedchamber that had been assigned to them. Beatrice, the flustered innkeeper had informed Fletcher earlier, had retired to her own quarters earlier, complaining of a sick stomach, a scrap of information the innkeeper had imparted to explain why the buxomy barmaid was not there to personally escort them to their room, which was a personal triumph for Billy, who had the comfort of knowing that her tall tale had successfully routed the woman.

Strangely, or so she thought, it also made her happy to see that Beatrice's defection didn't seem to bother Fletcher in the slightest. Obviously Fletcher Belden was the sort that flirted with anything in skirts—probably out of habit or some such nonsense—but did not really have a penchant for consorting with chance-met barmaids.

They walked down the narrow hallway, the uneven floor of the old inn giving Billy fits as she readjusted the unwieldy bulk of their belongings. It appeared that Fletcher did not believe in leaving all creature comforts behind when he traveled. She nearly stumbled in the darkness, so that Fletcher at last reached out a hand to steady her, commenting dryly that Beatrice must be very sick to have been too overcome by her sudden illness to light the candles in the hallway, leaving her customers to curse the darkness as they searched for the doors to their rooms.

At last Fletcher stopped in front of a substantial-looking closed door and twisted the knob. He opened the door and took two steps inside, Billy directly behind him, eager to be rid of her bundles, before a loud male bellow from inside the room stopped them both in their tracks.

"What in bloody blazes! Who is that? How dare you come barging in here without so much as a by-your-leave?"

Billy peeked out from behind Fletcher's back to see—thanks to the light of a single candle burning beside the bed—the faint outline of a very large, nearly naked man who seemed to be hovering overtop a much smaller, bare-shouldered female figure. Although she had never before been privy to precisely what went on between a man and a woman in the privacy of their bedroom, she had a very good suspicion as to what Fletcher had interrupted—and whom he had interrupted in the act of engaging in it!

"Beatrice." Billy breathed the name softly, recognizing the barmaid's blond hair. Now this was sticky. It was one thing for Fletcher to dismiss Beatrice because the woman had become ill, or had belatedly discovered she had morals and had decided to dedicate her life to chaste poverty while serving lepers in far-off Africa or some such tripe, but it was something entirely different to see that the idiotic woman had rejected him for such an obviously inferior, bloated specimen as the man now burrowing beneath the covers.

Billy's apprehensive gaze flew to Fletcher's face. She

wondered how long it would be before he exploded in wrath, but her employer appeared to be most infuriatingly calm, if not even amused.

Fletcher had immediately upon entering the room recognized the man in the bed to be none other than one James Something-or-other Whittington. Whittington was a thoroughly unlovely man whose major—nay, sole—claim to fame was that he was second cousin thrice removed to the beleaguered Lady Helen Whittington, who was forced by conscience to invite him to at least one small party a Season.

Although his lapse was not deliberate, Fletcher did not at once share this information with his groom, who was still more than mildly concerned that things could get nasty.

In fact, so intrigued was Belden to see the very much married man *en flagrant délit* that he totally forgot his groom for a moment, and only belatedly whispered a quick order for Billy, who had noisily dropped the baggage to the floor in shock, to gather their belongings and remove them and his too-young, innocent eyes from the room.

"A thousand pardons, sir. Please accept my apologies," Fletcher said to Whittington, not retreating a step. Beatrice struggled to cover herself, but the fat man, who had fleetingly reminded Billy of a newly shorn sheep, had fallen onto his back, selfishly pulling the majority of the sheets along with him.

"You offer your apologies, sirrah?" Whittington bellowed once he had found his voice. "I cannot settle for your apologies. I will not settle for your apologies! I demand satisfaction. Do you hear me?"

Clearly, Fletcher thought, although I recognize

Whittington, he is incapable of seeing through the darkness to detect my identity, for, if memory served him correctly, the athletically inept Whittington could not with any certainty be counted upon to maim a wingless fly with fifty blows from a hammer.

"You demand satisfaction?" Fletcher responded, calmly removing Billy's clutching hands from his sleeve and winking his groom a silent warning. "My goodness. My knees are knocking together at the thought. Do you hear the bones, sir? They're positively rattling."

"And so they should be," Whittington blustered. "But be you coward or coxcomb, I demand satisfaction. It is a matter of honor."

"Ah, yes," Fletcher said, nodding. "You are a man of honor, then? But I must ask, are you also a man of moderation? Although I know I have committed a truly reprehensible solecism, sir, do you truly believe it warrants our spilling our respective claret in the innyard?"

"I most certainly do," Whittington blustered hotly, if not quite so hotly as he had before Fletcher had brought up the subject of bloodshed. "Now, who are you? I am James Smith, sir, and I insist you answer my challenge."

"Smith, you say?" Fletcher repeated quietly, as if thinking aloud. "There must be an epidemic of Smiths this year in the Lake District. Perhaps this past winter was too mild to kill them all off. No matter. I bid you good evening, Mr. Smith." Fletcher walked to the bottom of the bed, knowing that his face was now visible in the candlelight, watching as James Whittington's bulbous blue eyes widened in sudden recognition . . . and fright.

Beatrice, who had been cowering beneath the sheets, chose that moment to peek out, wide-eyed, from behind her woefully inadequate disguise.

Fletcher casually looked in the barmaid's direction, bowed low, and inquired silkily, "Ah, and you must be the ever so lovely Mrs. Smith, I presume? Smith, my compliments, sir. Your wife is most lovely—and such a perfect match for you."

As Billy choked on relieved laughter, her own tension eased, Fletcher spoke again. "Smith, I remain your servant, and I can only hope you might reconsider what you are suggesting, not that I should be so cowardly as to run off, you understand, if you were to remain adamant, but you do have Mrs. Smith here to consider, as well as all the little Smiths. Please feel free to call on me in the morning if you truly wish to renew your challenge. The name is Jones, by the by, Fletcher Jones. There seems to be a rash of ordinary names in the region, doesn't there? Ah, well, ta-ta for now. I shouldn't want you to keep Mrs. Smith waiting."

James Whittington "Smith," who was in the midst of babbling nearly unintelligible apologies for having overreacted to a simple error, "Ha-ha, such a silly business, and a mistake that anyone could make, don't you know," didn't call Fletcher back.

Once the door to the room was closed behind them, Fletcher looked down at Billy and said, "Let that be a lesson to you, Billy."

"Never open a door without knocking, sir?" Billy asked cheekily, grinning, for the sight of the occupants of the bed had been more amusing than sordid.

"No," Fletcher answered, thoughtfully picking up his own pack and heading down the hallway.

"Never believe a barmaid named Beatrice when she says she knows how to give very good service?" Billy persisted, skipping along behind him.

Fletcher peered at the number on the next door, satisfying himself that this time he had chosen the correct one, and placed a hand on the knob.

"No, again, Billy," he corrected without rancor. "The lesson is this: when trying to hoax somebody, never give the sadly uninspired name of Smith. It is entirely too obvious, which is what got you into trouble with me in the first place. And just think: if I had believed the lie you told me, you might even now have been trying to explain away a possible relationship to that unimaginative buffoon."

Billy couldn't help herself. The events of the past few minutes had been too delicious for Fletcher to possibly spoil the moment for her. She walked into the room, dropped her blanket roll on the floor, and collapsed into a chair, laughing until her sides ached. "Did you see his face? It was purple," she exclaimed, wiping her streaming eyes. "When he finally recognized you, he all but groveled on the floor, which I will be endlessly grateful he did not do, for he was fast losing his fight with Beatrice for the sheet, and we had already seen more of the man than anyone should. It must be above everything wonderful to be so feared, Mr. Jones."

Stepping over his groom's outstretched legs, Fletcher picked up a sulphur match and tinderbox in order to light a small brace of candles. "Yes, I suppose it is, now that you mention it. Now, if only I could find either a relative or a single employee of mine that shares Mr. James Smith's awe, I should be a happy man. But I believe I am doomed to be unappreciated by my own household. Tell me Billy, if you are sufficiently recovered from your unseemly bout of hilarity, would it be asking too much of you to pull off my boots?''

Both Billy's good humor and her feelings of camaraderie with Fletcher Belden disappeared so quickly it was hard to believe they had ever existed. ''Pull off your boots? You want me to pull off your boots? Why? Don't your knees bend?''

Fletcher was now sitting on the side of the bed, the episode with Whittington already forgotten. But he was still wondering, as he had been doing when he opened the wrong door, why he was so amused to know that his possible romantic dalliance had upset his groom. Fletcher looked across the room at Billy, who was sitting stock-still on the chair, a mulish expression on his face.

''Don't poker up on me, Billy,'' he warned evenly. ''I know that we have cried friends this afternoon, and I am aware that you were not really born into this world with the temperament to become the devoted servant of any man, but are, in fact, a young runaway gentleman unaccustomed to taking orders.

''However, you are in my employ at the moment—more's the pity, for, alas, you are at times a most tiresome brat—and we are going to have to continue to deal with each other until we return to Lakeview and I can prevail upon dearest Beck to take you home. Now, if you would please to come over here and pull off my boots so that I might get into bed, I should greatly appreciate it. Or would you rather I slept beside you with them on?''

Billy closed her eyes in silent agony, for Fletcher had just confirmed her worst suspicions. He actually expected them to sleep in the same bed. Why did he have to be so magnanimous as to refuse to follow through on his threat to have her bed down in the stables? And if he was going to be so bloody generous about the thing, why couldn't he have laid down the blunt for separate rooms?

Oh, how could she have been so stupid as to rout Beatrice? Worse, how could she have been so completely crack-brained as to tell him she was a young gentleman? If she had told him she was a lowly servant's son, she still could have been sent to tuck herself up safely somewhere in the stables. What was that saying about tangled webs?

"Billy, I'm still waiting. Or do you think you can accomplish the job from where you are standing?"

Billy searched her fertile brain frantically for some inspiration that would save her from the ignominious task. "Is there no bootjack in the room?" she asked hopefully.

"A bootjack?" Fletcher responded with all the proper horror any well-turned-out gentleman felt toward such contraptions. A gentleman might bed down with his horse when out hunting or in wartime. A gentleman might have to go days without shaving, even wear a shirt a second time. But scratch his beloved Hessians with a jack? Never! "I'll give you to the count of three, Billy," he threatened, lifting his right leg out straight in front of him, "and then I will use the jack to remove your ears."

Knowing she had lost this round, Billy sighed and approached the bed, looking down at the boot. Grabbing hold of it by both heel and toe, she leaned back, praying the dratted thing would cooperate by sliding off Fletcher's foot. She tugged and she tugged, but the boot didn't budge.

"If you are through acting the clown, Billy," Fletcher said at last, "perhaps we can get on with it. Now, turn around, straddle my leg, and let me help you."

Turn around? Present him with a view of her back? Straddle his leg? Straddle his leg! It was obscene. It was also—Billy knew, cursing him—inevitable. Pulling her loose smock down more fully over her hips, she lifted her right leg and stepped over Fletcher's, bringing his muscular calf up between her thighs. If it were possible for a person to die of shame, she'd be toes cocked on the floor within moments.

But the worst was yet to come. "All right, Billy, since it is obvious that you have never done this before, I shall continue with my instructions. Place one hand around the heel, if you please, and the other on the sole, just beneath the toe. And for God's sake, don't smudge the leather any more than you can help. Good. The leather is most probably already doomed to bear witness to your paw prints evermore. Yes, that's it. You follow instructions well once you deign to listen. Now, here we go!"

A split second later Billy felt the sole of Fletcher's left boot firmly against her derriere as that man pushed her forward. Another split second and she was sprawled facedown on the floor, the liberated boot between her legs.

"Oh, dear," Fletcher commiserated with such a total lack of feeling that Billy nearly flew up to scratch out his laughing eyes. "It seems I somehow forgot to tell you to expect my help, doesn't it? Ah, well, these things will happen. Are you ready for the second boot?"

She was going to kill him, slowly, so that she could savor every moment of his death. She was going to wait until he was asleep and pour an entire pitcher of cold, preferably dirty, water over his head. She was going to put a burr under Pagan's saddle and chortle gleefully as the stallion bucked Belden and his shiny Hessians off his back and straight into a mud puddle. She was . . . good God! She was going to have to feel his stockinged foot intimately placed against her hindquarters.

"I want to go home," she whined weakly, still sitting on the floor. "Please."

"The devil you say. An admirable sentiment, Billy, and exactly the one I had hoped this little sojourn through the district would elicit. I cannot express how overjoyed I am to know that I have convinced you to return to the bosom of your family. Aye, you may stare, and I shouldn't wish it bruited about—most especially to Beck, who is already wondering if I have misplaced my wits—but this entire trip has been in the way of a good deed, for I was determined to gain your confidence so that I might help you. However, we cannot possibly reach Keswick this evening, and, alas, I am still wearing one boot."

If she were to live to the age of one hundred—which she most probably wouldn't, for she knew she was going to hang for what she planned to do to the horrible Fletcher Belden—Billy would never again be so embarrassed. This was worse than the stop they had made in the woods, when only her fleetness of foot and carefully averted eyes had kept her from perishing of terminal humiliation on the spot.

Rising slowly to her feet, as if she were already mounting the thirteen steps to the gallows, Billy straddled Fletcher's outstretched left leg and gingerly placed her hands on his boot. She could feel the warmth of Fletcher's stockinged foot burning through the thin jersey of her breeches, and discern the imprint of all five of his toes searing a white-hot brand of shame into her buttocks.

He seemed to hesitate, his foot shifting slightly, first this way, then that way, as if measuring the softness of the flesh beneath him, while Billy held her breath, tears stinging her eyes, before Fletcher finally gave a mighty heave that sent Billy and the second boot to the floor.

It was over. She had done it. She looked up at Fletcher, searching his eyes for any hint that he had known that the buttocks he had recently known so intimately were not that of a young boy, but the man looked to be faintly confused rather than suspicious, and she breathed a sigh of relief.

She shook her head, wordlessly berating herself for her fears. Fletcher Belden's sensibilities weren't so subtle, so discerning. He wouldn't have been intrigued by a soft bottom. It took the bosom of someone like Beatrice, a bosom so prominent she could have just as easily balanced the mugs of ale on it, leaving her hands free for other work, to pique the man's interest.

Billy stayed on the floor to tug off her own boots, then walked around to the opposite side of the bed, intent on getting herself between the covers, her back turned to Fletcher, before that man decided to strip to the buff, which she prayed to the good Lord he was not in the custom of doing.

"You intend to sleep in your breeches?" Fletcher asked just as Billy raised the covers and made to slide beneath them.

"You didn't give me time enough to pack another

set of clothes," she answered gruffly, wondering to herself if Fletcher had now set himself in the role of her guardian or, even worse, her mother. "I'll change my linen in the morning, if that's all right with you."

There was a short, pregnant silence, during which Billy prayed to any kind saint who might still be awake and prone to listen to her, that Fletcher would accept her explanation and be done with it.

"Suit yourself," Fletcher said at last, already in the process of ridding himself of every stitch of clothing he wore before he, too, slid between the covers. "I never did know a boy your age who did not have a great affection for filth. Just stay on your own side of the bed, if you please."

Billy knew Fletcher was naked without having to look at him, a thing she would rather have died than do. She knew he was naked because an hour later, as she was still desperately trying to find sleep, Fletcher turned toward her, one long arm snaking out to wrap itself around her waist.

She tried to move him away, for his body was curved against her spine, her fingers tingling as she encountered his bare forearm. Turning fully onto her back, she looked across the pillow straight into Fletcher's sleeping face. The bright light of the full moon streaming through the windowpanes detailed every feature that lay so close to her, and her skin was cooled by the sweet breeze of his slow, even breathing.

He was so incredibly, heart-stoppingly handsome, a fact that had occurred to her before, but without causing the reaction it was causing now. The covers, which had somehow slipped to his waist, moved slowly up and down with his every breath, and she swallowed hard, averting her eyes from what she knew to be forbidden territory, only to be captured by the sight of his finely muscled chest.

His hair was blond there as well, as blond as the hair on his head, and shone almost silver in the moonlight. She had seen men stripped to their waists before—a person couldn't live in the district and not see workmen in the fields, their shirts discarded as they worked with the sheep—but she had never been this close to one of them.

It was not just his chest that was bare—and she knew it. Oh, dear Lord, did she know it! She pushed at his arm again, but he only moaned softly, pressed the length of his body more intimately against hers, and tightened his grip.

How did she get to be in this terrible position? What madness had allowed her to continue her deception, so nobly begun, to such a degree? She firmed her jaw, remembering the events that had led up to her escape from Patterdale, trying to convince herself that she had been right to do what she had done, what she was still trying to do.

She had to know if Fletcher Belden was a good man, a man who would save her from the life her circumstances had thrust upon her, a life that could end at any moment as she became a sacrifice to the dark demons or whatever nonsense it was that her relatives were about.

But had she been correct? Had she really seen what she thought she had seen? Of course she had! How could she doubt it? Yes, she had a vivid imagination. Yes, that imagination had more than once landed her in the briars. She would have to be even more of a zany than her relatives thought her to be to deny it, even to herself. But that didn't mean she had been wrong this time.

Besides, she didn't have to stay in Patterdale, waiting for her relatives to do her in. She wasn't even supposed to be in Patterdale. Fletcher Belden was supposed to have come and taken her away.

But he hadn't come. She had waited and waited—for a whole long month—and he hadn't come. He hadn't written. He hadn't even sent someone else to act in his stead.

So, being a female of independent mind, she had come to Lakeview seeking him, only to find that he was kicking up his heels in London, totally insensitive to her plight.

It had been one thing to run from Patterdale, but it was another thing entirely to place herself in the hands of someone who so obviously did not want to deal with her.

Yet, knowing she couldn't possibly return to Patterdale without reaping the whirlwind of wrath her escape had doubtless stirred up, she had decided to remain at Lakeview incognito, to see and judge Fletcher Belden for herself, and then make up her own mind as to which was the lesser of two evils: Patterdale or Lakeview.

Yes, she had planned to see Fletcher Belden. She hadn't, however—she thought with a nervous giggle, wondering if she was well on her way to becoming hopelessly depraved—planned on seeing quite this much of him.

Fletcher moved again, his beautifully molded hand now traveling in a slow upward motion, toward her smock-covered breast. Billy froze, unable to move, as his fingers trailed lightly across the crest of one soft mound. He moaned softly, his hand gently cupping her breast, as a slight, satisfied smile curved the corners of his mouth. His lower body pressed even more provocatively against her hipbone.

This couldn't be happening! Billy couldn't breathe. She couldn't react.

But it was happening. And she was reacting. She was melting, she was burning. She was dying of embarrassment, she was dying of curiosity. Sensations she could not explain coursed white-hot through her body, bringing a flush to her cheeks and a faint buzzing to her ears.

Summoning up every bit of moral and physical strength remaining to her—and at the moment, there wasn't a lot there to draw on—Billy pushed his encroaching, intoxicating hand from her body and slid onto the carpet, leaving Fletcher to turn fully onto his stomach, a low, frustrated moan making her ache to pelt him repeatedly over the head with the pillow that had followed her off the bed.

Her body shaking with reaction, her heart pounding as she realized for the first time the full extent of what had nearly happened, Billy clutched the pillow to her and crossed to the window seat, where she spent the rest of the night curled into a small, miserable ball of pain and, perhaps, just a smidgen of regret.

Fletcher spent the better part of the following morning sneaking covert glances at his runaway-cum-groom as they rode toward Coniston. Something was wrong; some change had taken place between last night and today, but he couldn't put his finger on it.

He had slept well, or at least he thought he had, yet he had awakened curiously unrefreshed and somehow dissatisfied, as if he had gone to sleep thirsting for a woman and there had been no woman in his bed to quench that thirst.

He was a man of moderate needs, taking women as he found them, for pleasure, and without actively pursuing them with the ardor of someone like, say, a James Whittington. He had kept a mistress before his time in the Peninsula, and even his unrequited, unconsummated love for Christine Denham had not turned him away from the satisfactions to be found in a lovely woman's bed once Christine had been lost to him.

He'd had at least three women—three young, beautiful, willing women—since breaking off his courtship with Christine, so surely he had not been without a female for so long that he had been forced to dream about one. And, most certainly, he couldn't have wanted Beatrice enough to have dreamed about her embarrassingly overdeveloped charms.

So, why had he woken this morning so unsatisfied, feeling so cheated, with the memory of a desirable warm body melting against his floating so near the surface of his tormented mind?

Billy, now riding in front of him along a narrow winding path, had already been awake and fully dressed—his linen, Fletcher had hoped absently, already changed—when Fletcher had opened his eyes. It was strange, Fletcher remembered now. Billy had been looking at him oddly and had quickly turned his back when Fletcher made to throw back the covers and rise, the boy showing yet again his almost unseemly modesty.

Modesty? With another man? Was that what it had been? Or had it been more than that?

The silence of the open countryside, broken only by lowing cows and bleating sheep, was fractured as Fletcher suddenly exclaimed, "God's eyebrows! I couldn't have!"

Billy reined in her mount and turned to ask if something were wrong, but Fletcher didn't answer except to say that he had been thinking out loud.

He was too caught up in his waking nightmare—a nightmare that had a lot to do with the faint memory of holding Billy close against him during the night—to say more. From that nightmare it was only a short, uncomfortably breached gap to the memory of Billy's soft, slightly flared buttocks against his stockinged foot as the groom had helped him with his boots.

Billy was a most handsome young lad, fine-boned nearly to femininity, graceful, intelligent, and obviously born of good stock. He was appealing, too, in an infuriating way, what with his outrageously disrespectful behavior and almost imperial manner. Yes, Billy was very likable.

But, no. No! It was impossible. It was more than impossible—it was unthinkable. He couldn't be . . . He couldn't be lusting after a young boy.

Could he?

They climbed to the top of the Old Man of Coniston, leaving their horses behind at the Low Water Tarn, arriving at the summit just after midday.

The view from the Old Man was dazzling, and Billy was properly impressed, listening as Fletcher pointed out Skiddaw and the rugged fells to the north, peering carefully to the east as Fletcher directed her to look past Coniston Water to the Yorkshire hills in the background, exclaiming in glee as she could make out the sea and the Isle of Man to the west, and nodding in acknowledgment as she followed the direction of Fletcher's pointed finger to see through a gathering mist to the summit of Snowdon to the south.

It was the mist and their growing hunger that at last prompted them to abandon their scenic vantage point at the top of the fell and return to the horses, Fletcher once more subdued and Billy once more eyeing him warily, wondering just how much the man really remembered of the events of the past evening.

Retracing their steps until they reached a wider path, Fletcher led the way with Pagan, neither employer nor groom speaking, passing through Tilberthwaite, Fell Foot, and Yewdale, to finally cross the beck and turn to the left to what Fletcher said was Tilberthwaite Gill, a small, secluded gorge that had a force, or waterfall, at its upper end. It was beside the waterfall that Fletcher dismounted, announcing they would camp here for the night.

To Billy's tortured mind, Fletcher couldn't have made a worse choice. The small gorge was beautiful, even romantic—if one was of a mind to be romantic, which Billy most certainly was not. The waterfall, a lovely thing that danced and sang and gaily reflected the sunlight, drew her to its edge, to stand entranced as the slight spray dampened her cheeks and hair. Wildflowers and exotic grasses were everywhere, and birdsong filled the trees.

If Fletcher picked any of those wildflowers and formed them into a daisy chain, she would dunk him head and ears in the beck, for the last thing she needed was to see Fletcher Belden again at his heart-melting best. Would this terrible trip ever be over?

They would return to Lakeview in the morning. Fletcher had told her that as he had tied a bundle of food on his saddle and directed her to follow him out of the village of Ambleside in preparation of their ascent of the Old Man, one of his favorite climbs.

All that remained to be gotten through was the night, a night Fletcher planned to spend beneath the stars. He had been different today than he had been on their first day out. Not that he hadn't been nice to her, for he had been, but Billy sensed a strain between them that Fletcher had made no move to breach. And he was acting so manly! Unrolling her blanket to begin making herself a bed as far from Fletcher as she could without encouraging his wrath, Billy paused, sitting back on her haunches, and nodded a single time. Yes, that was it. Fletcher was trying to act manly, and her female heart had been in constant danger of being destroyed by his recitation of disgustingly manly exploits.

He had been talking about his adventures in town, times he had been out on the strut with his cronies. He had made a point—or so it seemed now—of telling her how many rounds he had gone with Gentleman Jackson. He had all but bragged about the Covent Garden warbler he'd had in keeping before leaving for the Peninsula "to fight Boney as any real man would," to quote him exactly.

As a matter of fact, Billy thought now, if Fletcher were to challenge her to a bout of arm-wrestling, just to show her how very manly he was, she wouldn't even blink. She sat front once more, tugging a corner of the blanket until she was happy with the way it lay, then sighed. Men. Who could understand them?

"Comfortable?" Fletcher asked, coming up behind her, having just finished tending to their mounts. "I thought I'd rough it a bit more myself, maybe just stretch out on the ground, with some of this dry grass to cover me. We had it a lot rougher than this on the Peninsula, you know."

"I know," Billy answered sharply, for she had just about had enough of his silliness. "Does this mean you'll be forgoing the meat pies you got for us in Ambleside so that you can find your dinner in the wilds? I hear some people think tree bark is quite palatable, although I don't know if you have to cook it in salted water first to remove the bugs."

Fletcher squatted, attacking his blanket roll so that it fairly exploded open in front of him, his linen and personal items spread out for all to see. Cursing, he gathered up his things, tucking them behind him, and stretched out on the blanket before answering. "No, brat, I don't think tree bark shall ever become part of my diet, although I could work up an appetite for rabbit, if I had thought to bring my gun. As it is, we shall have to make do the best we can with the pies from the inn. Do you hunt?"

The question, which Fletcher had seemed to add as an afterthought, took Billy by surprise. "No," she answered, shaking her head. "I never learned how. Do you?" she added fatalistically, knowing he was leading her into another "manly" discussion but feeling so strangely sorry for him that she did it anyway.

Fletcher idly began picking wildflowers, then abruptly stopped, as if suddenly realizing what he was about, and tossed the flowers into the bushes. ''I am not a dedicated hunter, if that's what you mean,'' he answered. ''Not since Beck and I were children. There's just so much civilization and rules involved in hunting among grown-ups, you understand.''

''Civilization?'' Billy questioned, not understanding but sensing that Fletcher was talking only to fill the silence—a silence she too wished to avoid. ''What sort of rules?''

Fletcher rolled onto his back, his hands clasped behind his head as he looked up into the still-light sky. ''When Beck and I were young, hunting was a game. We took only what we needed—small game, you understand—and ate what we shot.'' He turned his head to look at Billy. ''Did you ever hear of anyone eating a fox?''

Billy smiled, shaking her head, and reached into the basket to unearth the meat pies. ''But I have heard of foxes eating chickens, and sheep, and all sorts of farm animals. Surely you aren't against fox-hunting? They're vermin and the bane of every landowner.''

Fletcher accepted one of the meat pies. ''Thank you. No, Billy, I don't object to shooting foxes. It is the civilized method that perturbs me. And I don't just mean the obvious rules, such as not shooting one's host, one's host's hounds, any other dogs, or lastly, keepers and beaters, the keepers and beaters being not quite so important to the exercise but still not to be considered a fair trophy.''

''Not to mention being terribly hard to carry home in a sack or mount on the wall of the study,'' Billy put in, relaxing for the first time that day.

''Exactly, for that is the way all dedicated fox-hunters

think. Just consider the logistics of the thing, Billy. Thirty men on horseback—thirty men who are almost always the worse for drink, hurtling their mounts pell-mell over the countryside behind a slobbering passel of baying, fox-crazy hounds—and all to capture and rend limb from limb one tiny red animal. I just can't call that sporting—not unless we can find some way to arm the foxes."

Billy closed her eyes and had a sudden vision of a small army of foxes, their hind legs easily fitting astride immense hunters, blunderbusses tucked in their front paws as their pointed ears and long noses twitched and their black eyes twinkled, on the alert for their two-legged quarry. This was followed by a second vision of that quarry: a red-coated covey of large-bellied, tipsy fox-hunters, scampering across the fields on all fours, their tongues hanging from their mouths as they huffed and puffed in fear, a pack of hounds nipping at their heels.

Surely she should share this vision with Fletcher. Laughing, she reached across the blanket to lay a hand on his arm, to gain his attention.

Fletcher pulled his arm away as if stung, got to his feet, and turned his back to her. "I think I'm going to take a walk before I eat," he said, already moving away from her.

"But the meat pie is not going to last forever and should be eaten soon," Billy pointed out, looking up at his departing back in confusion. Fletcher's mood, which had been running hot and cold all day, had gone suddenly cold again as she had reached out to touch him. There could be only one reason.

It was her. Something had happened last night at the

inn that had made him dislike her, she decided as Fletcher disappeared down the path, leaving her behind with nothing but the birds and the falling water to keep her company.

"I guess he liked Beatrice more than I thought he did," she mumbled to herself, looking down at the meat pie, her appetite gone. "And it's such a pity, for I am beginning to believe I could like Fletcher Belden very much."

5

The fire Fletcher had built still burned steadily as he and Billy sat across from each other, lost in thought. The silence, broken only by the cheerful babbling of the brook, might have been comfortable if it weren't for those thoughts: Billy nervously remembering her reaction to Fletcher's touch, and a shaken Fletcher doing his best to banish his treacherous feelings from his tortured brain.

"Mr. Belden?"

"What?"

She hesitated, wondering what to say now that she had opened her mouth, her eagerness to break the silence outstripping her preparation for what would come next.

"Well, what?" Fletcher's voice sounded strained, his tone curt, and he sighed and added more gently, "You're feeling bored, I suppose. I understand. It isn't every man who appreciates a good silence."

Instantly, as had become usual since meeting this man, Billy felt her hackles rise. How could Fletcher Belden be so boorish as to tell her how she felt? He didn't know how she felt; he couldn't know. And how did she feel? Billy thought about that for a moment, then hung her head.

She felt stupid—that's how she felt. Stupid and childish, dressed up like some youthful urchin, itching in places she didn't know she had, and willing to give up her only hope of heaven for an hour-long soak in a hot tub. Lord, but she had grown heartily sick of breeches.

She also felt guilty. Guilty for deliberately deceiving Fletcher as to her true identity, and guilty because she wasn't such a simpleton that she hadn't, in the past few uncomfortable hours, figured out that Fletcher believed himself attracted to her and was most probably, even at this moment, damning himself as perverse. For all her slight build, which allowed her to pass for a young lad, she had, after all, passed her eighteenth birthday and could lay claim to some wits. No wonder Beatrice had fled into the arms of the portly James Smith!

Well, it was time and enough to set things right. She had set out to get to know Fletcher, not drive him to distraction. Billy sat up, crossing her legs, determined to make a clean breast of things and have done with this farce. She'd feel much better once the truth emerged into the open. Besides, maybe then they could return to Lakeview, where there was bound to be a tub.

"Mr. Belden, I—I—" she began hastily, then faltered.

"Yes?" Fletcher lifted his head, the dimple in his right cheek flashing as he smiled. "What's the matter? And please don't tell me you were wondering how to ask me if you might disappear into the trees again to relieve yourself. I never saw such modesty. You may as well be a woman, Billy, for all your missish ways."

Billy's jaw dropped in astonishment, all thought of confession evaporating in her brain at the wretched mistiming of Fletcher's verbal jab. How could the odious man say such embarrassing things, talking down to her as if she were some knock-in-the-cradle baby? How could she possibly say anything after that lowering remark?

"No," she blurted at last, glad it had grown dark enough to hide her red cheeks. "That wasn't at all what I had intended to ask," she added, shaking her head. "I just thought we could talk, that's all."

"Talk," Fletcher repeated, astonished once more by Billy's modesty. He couldn't wait to return to Lakeview and be shed of the boy—and his traitorous thoughts. But maybe Billy had the right idea. Talking would help pass the hours, for one thing, and give Fletcher less time to consider his feelings. "Very well. What would you like to talk about?"

Billy began slowly shaking his head, as if the action would jolt loose some inspiration. "Um . . . um . . . I don't know. London? Yes, that's good—we could talk about London. I've never been, you know."

"You haven't?" Fletcher asked blandly. "I would never have known, what with all the air of sophistication and town bronze you have about you." He withdrew a thin cheroot from his pocket and leaned forward to light it in the flames, not knowing how close he was to disaster, as Billy was once more harboring an urge to murder him. "And what would you like to know about London?"

Wasn't it enough that she had given him a general topic? Did she now need to be specific? Had the man no imagination of his own? London. It was a simple subject—a worldly man such as he should be able to prose on about it for hours with no prodding from her. Did she have to think of everything?

"I don't know," she said. "Beau Brummell," she all but shouted, suddenly inspired. "Yes, I should like to hear all about Beau Brummell."

Fletcher flopped over onto his back, smiling at Billy's innocent curiosity. Poor Beau. He had been doomed to evermore be the center of attention, even of small boys from the Lake District. After thinking silently for a few moments more, Fletcher quoted, " 'Oh ye! who so lately were blythesome and gay, at the butterfly's banquet carousing away; your feats and your revels of pleasure are fled, for the soul of the banquet, the butterfly's dead!' "

"What?" Billy looked toward the bottle of wine Fletcher had been sipping from all evening, wondering if the man had grown bosky. "What on earth is that?"

"That, my little friend," Fletcher responded, turning onto his side and raising up his head on one propping hand, "is 'The Butterfly's Funeral.' Beau wrote it about a dozen years ago, when he wallowed in some muse-ridden frame of mind, I suppose. There may be more verses, I cannot quite remember now, but that much has always stayed with me. I have wondered many times if he had some premonition about his falling out with Swellfoot and wrote the poem in order to be ready for it. Of course, just whom he intended cast in the role of Butterfly remains his secret."

Billy found herself interested in spite of herself. "Why doesn't the Prince Regent like Mr. Brummell anymore? They were the greatest of good friends for a long time, weren't they?"

Fletcher puffed on the cheroot, remembering all the tales he had heard about Beau and Prinny. He chuckled aloud. "Almost twenty years, if I'm right, dating all the way back to Beau's time in the Tenth Light

Dragoons.'' He shook his head. ''I doubt the dragoons ever recovered from the insult.''

''Insult? I don't understand. What did Mr. Brummell do?''

Fletcher held the cheroot in front of him, gazing into the red tip. ''No more than he had to, actually,'' he said, chuckling once more. ''As a matter of fact, poor Beau got himself so caught up with the social whirl of London and Brighton that he had difficulty finding his place for the parade, having been unable to commit his troop number to memory. Luckily, the man Beau stood directly in front of for parade was the possessor of a lovely—and quite enormous—blue nose, making it a simple thing for Beau to locate his place in line. Then misfortune struck and the game was up.''

''The blue-nosed man died?''

''No, much more than that,'' Fletcher explained. ''The blue-nosed man had gotten himself transferred to another group. Of course, as the blue-nosed man moved, so too did Beau, only to be informed by his superior officer that he had positioned himself in the wrong place. Beau, with, I am told, just the merest elevation of one eyebrow, turned to see the blue nose to his rear and stated firmly, 'Non-sense. I know better than that. A pret-ty th-ing, in-deed, if I did not know my own tr-oop.' ''

Billy laughed aloud at the mental picture Fletcher's words conjured. ''Is that how he sounds?'' she asked once her giggles were under control. ''What an odd way of speaking.''

''An affected drawl, I grant you, but although I should dislike it terribly in anyone else, Beau has always been able to bring it off beautifully.''

"And his dress," Billy pursued. "Is it true that he is copied by every man with any pretension to good grooming and fashion?"

"I have copied his simplicity most outrageously," Fletcher admitted unashamedly, for he had long admired his friend's unstated elegance and predilection for cleanliness, "although I have not gone so far as to spend hours tying a cravat or taken to bathing in milk. I can say that the air in London, never particularly healthful, has been greatly improved by Beau's oft-copied prescription for daily bathing and sparkling clean linen."

Billy, scratching at yet another itch, silently agreed with Beau's prescription. "Yet now he and the Prince Regent are quarreling. Poor Mr. Brummell. He must be terribly unhappy."

Fletcher, after tossing the remains of the cheroot into the flames, moved to recline against the trunk of a nearby tree. "He's resigned to it, I'd say," he said, reflecting on Beau as he'd last seen him. "Although he is gambling too high of late. He always did make a fine art of folly. I don't foresee a happy future for Beau, to tell you the truth, now that Swellfoot is known to no longer favor him. It's a damnable pity, for Beau—and not that fat, spendthrift, grandmother-chasing flawn—is truly the First Gentleman of Europe."

Sensing that Fletcher's mood had once more turned inward in the silence that followed his last words, Billy spoke again. "Mr. Brummell cannot be the only man of note in London. Tell me about the others."

Fletcher, who had been remembering Beau as he'd last seen him, playing too deep at White's and losing badly, found himself to be more than willing to change the subject. He told Billy of Henry Luttrell, whom he had seen that last day in town, making his groom laugh with tales of Henry's agile wit. Then he quoted Samuel Rogers, a man so thin his friends believed he most resembled a cadaver, on the subject of marriage: " 'It matters little whom a man marries, for he is sure to find the next morning he has married someone else.' "

Billy frowned at that disparaging male remark, the female in her struck. "That wasn't funny," she complained, shoving a stick into the fire. "What do London gentlemen do besides drink and gamble and poke fun at women? I should soon be bored with sitting in White's window, laughing at the people getting wet in the rain outside."

"Too tame for you, Billy-boy?" Fletcher questioned, remembering how bored he had been among the hustle and bustle of London society in full flight. "I tend to agree with you. Evenings can be the worst if one is not a dedicated gamester. Take rout parties, for instance."

Billy sat forward, for now Fletcher had indeed captured her interest. "Oh, yes, do tell me about rout parties. They sound like such fun."

"Fun?" Fletcher repeated, grimacing. "Billy, I've had more fun cleaning my teeth. No real conversation exists at a rout, no cards, no music, no dancing. It is nothing more than a woman's excuse to throw open her house and show off her furnishings. The hostess must, of course, invite at least three times the people able to stand shoulder to shoulder in her house at any one time, just so that she can tell all her friends that her party had been a 'veritable squeeze.'

"A guest spends at least an hour in his carriage, awaiting the moment his coachman can inch forward to the front door, then waits through another hour on the stairs in order to shake hands with the lady of the house. After that it is a matter of winding, sheeplike, from room to room, elbowing, twisting, turning, and winding through drawing room, saloon, bedroom, and salon, only to find oneself back on the threshold, totally winded and longing for the comfort of one's carriage, which, of course, is waiting at least three blocks distant. Rout parties—a pox on them!"

Billy felt herself fast becoming depressed. London was not at all as she had supposed it. "But what about the theater? Surely you must have something kind to say about London theater?"

"For young men?" Fletcher considered the thing a moment, wondering what aspect of theatergoing would most appeal to a young lad. "There is Fops Alley, I suppose. An enterprising gentleman can station himself there and then go behind between the acts to chat with the actresses, who can be most appreciative."

"Do you do that?" Billy frowned, not knowing why the thought of Fletcher cavorting with actresses distressed her. As a matter of fact, the thought of Fletcher being anywhere other than this secluded gorge, with anyone else but her, conjured up a most totally unlovely picture.

"I did, long ago in my grasstime. I've learned to appreciate what is going on out in front now that I am older. But we are talking of London in general, not myself in particular. And although I may be feeling a bit jaded at the moment, I must admit to there being plenty to do for a young fellow a few years older than you.

"There's boxing or fencing in Gentleman Jackson's,

or with Shaw the Lifeguardsman, for instance, or riding in the park, going out on the strut, or visiting friends. Dear Lord, there is no end to the visiting. A fellow could make a career of visiting, as Henry Luttrell has.'' And with that, Fletcher reached out, took up his hat, and placed it over his face, as if to signal that he was about to go to sleep.

Billy, feeling the beginnings of a cramp in her left leg, stretched herself out and dutifully tried to imagine London as Fletcher described it. It sounded nearly as boring as Patterdale, although there did seem to exist more for a person to do to bore her.

Then she brightened, remembering that Fletcher most probably had been trying to make London sound as unappealing as possible, in order to dissuade her from ever thinking of running off to such a place rather than meekly allowing herself to be led to a nasty aunt in Tunbridge Wells. And what a hum that story was! Surely a young woman could find more excitement in the metropolis.

Having so buoyed herself with that thought, she set out to learn more about Fletcher Belden, the man. ''Hedge said you fought in the Peninsula. Was it terribly exciting?''

Fletcher lifted the hat from his eyes and regarded Billy consideringly. What mischief could the boy be planning now in that fertile imagination of his—thoughts of running away to make a name for himself in the army? He smiled, knowing Billy would be fair and far out if he tried that. There'd be precious little room for downy-cheeked babies in a peacetime army.

''Exciting, did you say?'' Fletcher responded, flashes of memory flitting through his brain. Yes, he had to admit it, war could be exciting.

Billy shrugged, searching for another word. "Well, was it interesting? I mean, Hedge said you served with the duke. Surely it had to be wonderful to watch the great man in the field?"

Fletcher closed his eyes and thought about the Duke of Wellington. He laughed aloud as a sudden thought struck him. "He shaved himself. Every morning, no matter what. Shaved himself, packed his own things, and emerged dressed from his tent each morning before light. Try as I might, I never beat him."

He suddenly sobered. "And he never asked a man to do what he himself wouldn't. As a result, his men would do anything he asked. Yet, at the same time, at heart he despised the ranks, calling them the scum of the earth. Only when he wanted the impossible from them did he address them as 'my lads'—and then, by God, they'd do it for him. Not once, but a hundred times."

Billy bit her tongue as she realized she had been about to say something that would give her away, for she had learned all this and more about the Iron Duke long ago. "They trusted him to bring them through, I should imagine," she said, peering through the darkness to try to read Fletcher's expression.

"We all did," Fletcher agreed, allowing the hat to slide down over his eyes once more. "I can remember a night I rode the perimeter with Wellington and we approached the sentry on the way back into camp. Someone had changed the signal and neither the duke nor I knew the countersign. Imagine it—the commander-in-chief being denied admittance to his own camp. But I shouldn't have worried. The sentry, a good Irishman with the heart of a lion, took a look, snapped his musket to the salute, and piped up heartily, 'God bless yer crooked nose. I'd sooner see it than ten thousand men!' "

"That's wonderful! Tell me more," Billy pleaded, leaning forward, entranced.

"I asked him—twice, as I recall—and he just kept grinning and nodding, saying, *Sí*, *sí*, all but pushing the stick skewering the thing in my face. Now remember, I hadn't had meat or much of anything else in nearly two weeks, so I took a bite." Fletcher pulled a face at the memory of the taste that had nearly gagged him. "And that, my young friend, explains how I learned that 'rabbit' is not an international word."

Billy, lying on her side opposite Fletcher across the dying fire, a blanket across her hips, her head sleepily propped on one hand, asked companionably, "And what was it, really, if it wasn't rabbit? You said it looked like a rabbit."

Fletcher shifted slightly as he reclined against a tree trunk, at his ease for the first time since awakening that morning.

How he had allowed himself to be gotten on the subject of his days in the Peninsula he didn't remember—probably in yet another attempt to convince himself he was a man to the tips of his boots and couldn't possibly be physically attracted to a young lad of no more than thirteen. But he had spent the last two hours happily reminiscing about a period in his life he had once believed he could never remember with any degree of fondness.

He smiled at a widely yawning Billy as he positioned a hand behind his head. "I never had the courage to ask, halfling, but I can tell you this much: I never heard a dog bark for the three days we were in that village.''

''That's terrible! But you didn't eat it,'' Billy declared positively, no longer appearing to be the least bit sleepy.

''I have dazzled you, no doubt.'' Fletcher grinned wickedly. ''Let's just say I didn't mind sharing it with my men.''

''You did eat it?'' Billy felt her stomach turn at the thought. ''You and your men ate a dog? How could you? I would much rather have starved.''

Fletcher leaned his head back to gaze up at the stars that dotted the clear night sky, then looked across the fire at Billy's stricken expression. ''Oh, halfling, but I would much rather have not. War deals harshly with refined sensibilities.''

''I suppose you're right,'' Billy muttered halfheartedly as she felt very drowsy and wasn't really listening with more than half an ear. She pushed herself up, fighting off sleep, to sit cross-legged, her hands on her knees, for the night had been going so well that she hated for it to end. ''Tell me another story, please—but another funny one, like the one you told me about the beauty competition your friend held, giving the prize to the village girl who had the most teeth.''

''William Darley?''

Billy fell suddenly silent, for Fletcher had succeeded in riveting her full attention. ''Who?'' she breathed, feeling as if a large rock had just settled in her stomach.

''William Darley,'' Fletcher repeated, looking at Billy oddly. ''Hadn't I mentioned his name? He was the best of good fellows, Billy-boy—a gorgeous man and the very devil of a bruising soldier. Sat a horse beautifully, too, as I recall. Saved my bacon a time or two as well. Damn, but I miss that lovable bastard. What a waste!''

"A waste? Wh-what happened to him?" Billy could barely get the words past her suddenly dry lips as she looked at Fletcher piercingly.

Fletcher took a long pull on the cheroot, allowing the exhaled smoke to slowly escape his mouth to rise in a wreath over his blond head. What had happened to William? What always happened to the good ones, the caring ones, the ones whose heart and mind could not accept the carnage taking place all around them? "He died," he said at last, his voice terse.

"H-how?"

Would the boy never have enough? Fletcher sighed, reluctantly allowing the memory to overtake him. "The fighting had worn down for the day, finally, after a great cost on both sides. It had been a long day, ever since dawn, when one of the men on the perimeter had called out that we'd better look sharp because Old Trousers was coming."

"Old Trousers? Did he mean Wellington? I know the men had a lot of nicknames for the duke."

Fletcher laughed mirthlessly. "No, it wasn't the duke. The French *pas de charge*, their forward movement, made a rub-a-dub noise, so when they approached we could hear them. It sounded like trouser legs rubbing together."

"Oh," Billy said quietly. "So it was a large battle?"

Fletcher repositioned the cheroot from one side of his mouth to the other with a deft movement of his tongue. "We won—or at least we lost fewer men than the French. We were tending to our wounded, and William went back out onto the field to search for survivors. We heard a shot, turned, and saw him fall." His gray eyes dulled. "One of the frogs wasn't quite dead, you see, and decided to take one more Englishman with him into hell. I obliged him somewhat by personally speeding him on his way."

"You killed the frog—the French soldier?"

The gray eyes snapped furiously. "What would you have had me do—congratulate him for his splendid aim? Grow up, Billy. Of course I killed him, and I don't regret it. William wasn't dead when I got to him, but he died a few hours later, back in camp, without ever speaking. It was the most extraordinary thing."

"Extraordinary?" Billy could feel herself dying inside, but she had to hear it all.

The tip of the cheroot glowed bright red as Fletcher drew on the other end. "When I carried William into camp there was no room to lay him among the injured. A soldier, one of Wellington's 'scum of the earth,' and dying himself of too many wounds to count, saw William as I laid him on the stones outside the tent. The soldier, who had a filthy straw palliasse to lie on, shoved himself over to make room for his superior officer. He said . . . he said he couldn't die in peace while the lieutenant colonel lay on stones. William Darley inspired that kind of loyalty."

Billy swallowed hard, stifling a sob. She brushed quickly at the tears that blinded her, and made a great business of lying down, pulling the blanket up to her chin. "Good night," she mumbled, unable to say more. The evening had lost all its charm, and she turned her back, praying for sleep.

Fletcher only grunted, moving the cheroot back to his mouth, knowing he wouldn't find any more sleep this night.

* * *

"What in thunder are you about now?" Fletcher called out as he thought he espied Billy's slight form cowering behind a tree. Dawn had just broken and he was lying on his side, cold, and still thoroughly out of sorts. He had slept, obviously, but it couldn't have been for long and it hadn't improved his mood.

"What do you think I'm about? I'm getting dressed," Billy shot back belligerently, hopping about on one foot as she struggled into her left boot. Drat the man! How could he be so sound asleep one moment and so annoyingly awake the next?

"Can it really be necessary for you to hide, Billy?"

"*Eeek*!" Billy whirled about, for Fletcher's voice had come from directly behind her, and since she had been off-balance, she promptly fell on her rump. "How dare you sneak up on me like that?" she demanded, glaring up at him while simultaneously groping for her jacket. Thank heaven she had saved her boots for last and was decently covered.

"Sneak up on you?" Fletcher bellowed, losing control. Enough was enough! "You're the one who's always sneaking about. What's the matter with you, Billy? Why do you think you have to hide from me? Is there something wrong with you, or do you think I'm the one with the problem?"

Billy scurried backward on her hindquarters until she collided with a tree trunk that effectively halted her retreat. She swallowed down hard on her fear, for she could admit to being genuinely frightened by the strange, almost haunted look in Fletcher's eyes. "I—I don't know what you mean," she stammered, hating the way her voice seemed to crack on the last word. "Wh-what could be wrong with us?"

Fletcher stared down on his trembling groom for a long, heart-stopping moment, then shook his head. "Nothing, halfling," he said, his voice suddenly weary. "Nothing at all. I'm sorry if I frightened you." He turned away, heading back toward the now-cold fire. "I'll leave you alone to finish dressing. But please hurry, for I am determined to reach Lakeview as soon as possible."

"Then we're definitely heading back this morning?" Billy asked, hurriedly pulling on her second boot so that she could follow Fletcher. "I had rather hoped . . ."

Fletcher stopped, turning slowly to look down at his groom. "Yes? You had rather hoped for what, halfling?"

Billy opened her mouth, but found that she couldn't speak. What had she hoped? She had hoped for an end to this ill-advised excursion. She had hoped to learn more about Fletcher and, after their talk last night, more about William Darley. She had hoped to find a way to tell Fletcher what she knew she wanted to tell him, had to tell him. "You mentioned a small competition with the horses," she said at last, mentally flaying herself for being the worst sort of coward.

Fletcher eyed her dispassionately before turning away to begin packing up his belongings, and Billy's heart ached for him. She knew what mayhem had to be taking place in his mind, could sympathize for his inner torment, for she was beginning to experience the same exciting pull between them that he must be feeling—and cursing himself for feeling. Why hadn't she said what she felt in her heart? Why couldn't she bring herself to confess her true identity, make a clean breast of things, so that they could make a new beginning?

"It's too late," she murmured aloud, knowing that she had waited too long, held her tongue a day more than she should have, and thus lost any chance she might have of ever telling Fletcher Belden the complete truth.

"Too late?" Fletcher had heard her. He looked up at the brightening sky. "It's not too late, Billy, not if you think you can live without breakfast. Come on, help me saddle the horses, and we can be off."

"You'll really race me?" Billy stood stock-still a moment, then exploded into action, grabbing at her blanket and running off toward She-Devil. Fletcher Belden really was the nicest man she had ever met—except for William, naturally. "You'll have to give me a head start, of course," she pointed out, hefting the saddle onto the mare's back. "It wouldn't be fair, else."

"Of course," Fletcher answered from Pagan's back, watching as Billy searched about for a rock to stand on in order to mount. "We'll wait until we're on more level ground, then have at it."

Billy brought She-Devil into line behind Pagan as they walked the horses back toward the main road, looking over her shoulder to bid a silent farewell to the small waterfall and the brook that babbled along happily, unaware of the part they had played in helping to make the past night both the happiest and yet the most unsettling in Billy's short lifetime.

There was nothing else for it, Billy decided as they made their way to the floor of the valley. She would have to leave. Disappear. Go away. Never looking back. The truth could only hurt her now. Fletcher would hate her for her deception, for making a fool of him. Either that, or he'd murder her!

"This looks good," Fletcher said, breaking into Billy's depressing thoughts. He raised a hand to point to a five-barred gate in the distance. "From here to the fence, halfling, and I'll count to ten before I start. Fair enough?"

Billy smiled at him, her heart melting. He could be so very nice. After all, as far as Fletcher knew, she was only his groom, and yet he insisted upon treating her as his equal. "More than fair," she answered, forgetting her plans to best him in the race, by fair means or foul.

"And don't be sawing at the mare's mouth," Fletcher warned just as he raised his hand to give Billy the signal to start.

Her eyes narrowed, all her good feelings for the man evaporating under the heat of her sudden anger. He never could leave well enough alone, could he? He always had to ruin the moment by saying something totally unnecessary. Of course she wouldn't saw at She-Devil's mouth. What did he think she was? Some cow-handed bungler? Well, she'd show him!

"To the other side of the gate," she yelled as Fletcher's hand came down, and urged She-Devil into an immediate gallop, knowing the mare's hooves would throw up large clumps of sod directly into Pagan's face.

Pagan, unused to being left in the dirt, immediately reared, keeping Fletcher occupied in trying to settle his mount a full five seconds past the agreed-upon count of ten. Billy had raced far ahead of him by the time he and Pagan could take up the chase, Fletcher cursing fluently under his breath as he planned what he would do to his groom once he caught him—if the damn fool idiot didn't break his neck attempting an impossible jump.

Billy didn't have to look back over her shoulder to know that Fletcher was gaining on her; she could hear the pounding of Pagan's hooves, even above the hurtful pounding of her own heart. Leaning forward into She-Devil's neck, she urged the mare to more speed even as she knew the mount wouldn't be equal to the five-bar jump.

Maybe it would be best this way, Billy thought with her usual dramatic flair. She could break her neck in a fall and never have to worry about what she would do with the rest of her life. Fletcher would find her limp, lifeless body on the other side of the gate, gather her into his arms, weeping buckets at her tragic demise, discover that she was really a woman, and . . . discover that she was really a woman! What could she be thinking about?

She couldn't let him discover that she was a woman—not that way! The thought was much too embarrassing, even for a corpse. She shot a look to her left, the open countryside that beckoned. No, it wouldn't be possible. She couldn't outdistance Pagan. She'd only be caught and punished for a horse thief. They'd put her in the dock, torture her, and find out that she was a woman . . . There was that awful thought again!

Billy hazarded a peek over her shoulder and saw Fletcher coming up hard behind her, his arm outstretched as if he meant to pluck her from the saddle before she could put She-Devil to the gate. He was going to rescue her. What a lovely thought! How noble Fletcher could be, how heroic. He would swoop down on her, hoist her from the saddle, hold her trembling body close against his chest, and discover that she was a woman.

Billy's head reeled in disbelief. How did she manage to get herself into predicaments like this? Life wasn't supposed to be this difficult.

Even the hapless heroines in the novels she read under the covers at night never had such problems. All they had to deal with were headless specters, groaning ghosts, and evil demons. They never had to worry about taking care of personal needs behind a tree, or trying to sleep with a naked man beside them, or choosing between nefarious relatives and a breathtakingly handsome man who hadn't cared enough about her to come seeking her on his own but would rather roam the countryside with a groom he, in his kindness, was rapidly driving to distraction.

Suddenly, the time for indecision and self-pity had passed. Pagan had drawn nearly abreast of the mare, Fletcher riding so close beside her that Billy could hear him breathing. She had to make a choice. Her options had narrowed to either certain death in the jump, or near certain death by embarrassment in Fletcher's arms.

Fate, that dubious lady who had been decidedly unkind to Billy in the past few months, took this time to rear her head, in the form of a small hole. Pagan's right front hoof was rudely introduced to the hole, and both horse and rider went crashing to the ground in an instant; leaving Billy to rein in the mare, dismount, and race to Fletcher's side as he lay, stunned, on the soft sod.

"Oh, don't be dead, please don't be dead," Billy keened, cradling Fletcher's head in her lap as she rocked back and forth, knowing the accident had been entirely her fault. "You can't be dead. Look, there's Pagan, back on his feet and none the worse for his tumble. If a stupid horse can be all right, so can you. Please, Fletcher, speak to me. Please speak to me."

"What do you want me to say?"

"Fletcher!" Billy nearly gave in to the urge to shower his face with grateful kisses, only saving herself at the last moment, saying, "I knew you'd be all right, Mr. Belden, sir. It wasn't a bad fall."

Fletcher, from his oddly comfortable position on the ground, his head still resting in Billy's lap, blinked once and asked, "Pray tell me what, in your obviously twisted mind, would constitute a bad fall? I haven't been unhorsed since I was twelve. It wasn't a particularly pleasant experience then, and it isn't any more palatable now. Never mind. I can see by that puzzled look on your face that I have asked a silly question. I hope you don't object, Billy, but I'm going to ask another one. Would you mind releasing the death grip you've got on my skull so that I might try to get up and see to my horse?"

"You're not angry?" Billy queried, still keeping her hands positioned on either side of his head. "You're not going to hit me or anything, are you?"

"Hit you? And why would I do that?" Fletcher questioned, his voice a quiet purr.

Billy could think of any number of reasons why Fletcher Belden should like nothing better than to beat her into a jelly, but she wasn't about to gift him with any of them. "No reason," she said, shrugging, and released him.

The next thing she knew, Billy lay facedown across Fletcher's knees and he was delivering a half-dozen stinging slaps to the rear of her breeches. "That's for talking back to me at every turn," he said, spanking her for the first time. "And these two are for lying to me about who you really are," he told her, bringing his hand down twice more.

"Ow! Stop it," Billy cried, desperately trying to cover her rump with her hands.

"And this one is for damn near killing yourself with your stupid, headstrong stunt," he went on doggedly, pushing her hands away. "And these are for damn near killing me!"

Tears stung at Billy's eyes as Fletcher unceremoniously dumped her onto the ground and stood up, calling to Pagan, who immediately raised his head from the clump of grass he had been nuzzling and walked over to his master.

"You can't just leave me here," Billy whined, wiping at her runny nose as she looked up at the monster that had once been William Darley's best friend.

Fletcher refused to look at his groom. He couldn't look at him, not without letting Billy see the self-disgust on his face. It had happened again, dammit! He had only delivered a long-overdue spanking to an insufferable, willful brat of a child. So, why was he feeling that same, now familiar surge of frustrated passion that had first struck him when he woke up at the inn?

His hand tingled at the memory of its contact with Billy's well-rounded buttocks. His loins throbbed with a longing that proved more damning than exciting. His mouth had gone dry, his heart pounded painfully, his legs were unsteady—and none of his reactions had anything to do with his spill from Pagan.

"I'm not going to leave you, halfling," he said at last, his voice gentle, but still not daring to look at his groom. He rounded up She-Devil and brought the mare close by so that Billy, making use of Fletcher's cupped hands, could boost herself into the saddle.

"I—I'm sorry," Billy whispered hoarsely, sniffling, once she sat astride the mare, her abused buttocks stinging as she moved about, trying to find a halfway comfortable spot. "I didn't mean any harm. Truly."

Fletcher looked up at his groom, his features drawn and pale. He couldn't really be angry with Billy. It wasn't Billy's fault that he, Fletcher Belden, despised himself very much at the moment.

All Fletcher's thinking centered on returning to Lakeview, sending Billy off to his aunt in Tunbridge Wells as soon as humanly possible, and finding himself a willing woman—any willing woman—so that he could make himself believe he hadn't turned into some sort of twisted monster. "I know you didn't, halfling," he said kindly, turning away just as the skies opened and a drenching rain descended on the valley. "Now, let's go home."

6

"Fletch, can this woebegone creature I'm seeing really be you? Lethbridge told me you were back. You look terrible—even worse than you did in London. I thought you went away for a rest, yet I've seen you looking fresher after a three-day bout with the bellyache. Don't let your aunt stumble on you looking like this, or she'll be trotting out some nasty physic, sure as check."

"A bellyache?" Fletcher repeated tonelessly, and slumped into a chair in his dressing room. "To tell you the truth, Beck, I believe I should welcome a bellyache at this moment, as it might serve to take my mind off this blasted headache."

"Sleeping outside isn't what it used to be, I imagine," Beck inserted playfully, shaking his head as Fletcher groaned.

"Never let it be said you'd ever delight in another man's misery, my friend. Do you think you could leave off gloating long enough to round up some brandy for me? Lethbridge gave me such a nasty look when I asked him to fetch some that I don't believe there'll be a decanter brought up here any time soon. Do you know, dear Beck, how lowering it feels to realize that I am no longer master in my own house?"

Beck closed and locked the door to the dressing room

before unearthing a decanter and two glasses from a nearby cabinet, and poured them each a drink.

"Your aunt has read some learned tome discussing the rising of ill humors in the liver caused, naturally, by demon drink. I believe Lethbridge to be only following her order that no spirits be served until the dinner hour, in the interest of health, you understand. But that's nothing to the point, old friend. Now, would you mind telling me why you look as if you've just been told the world's going to end tomorrow, just when you had extensive plans for next spring?"

Fletcher took the glass, draining it before holding it up to be filled once more. "When did you take to hiding the brandy, Beck? Surely you aren't afraid of my aunt."

Beck pointedly ignored the question as he refilled both glasses, not wanting his friend to know that he had indeed taken the path of least resistance, hiding away a supply of brandy rather than upsetting dear Miss Belleville, whose intentions, if not her ideas, were good. "Didn't you have any fun at all while you were haring back and forth across the countryside, communing with nature?"

Fletcher stared into the bottom of his glass, wanting to unburden himself to Beck but not knowing how to start, where to begin, if, indeed, there were anything he could say without damning himself. What could he say? Could he tell Beck that he had found himself attracted to his groom? Hardly.

Could he tell him that he had acted the buffoon, bragging about his exploits like some strutting rooster, just to soothe his unease at the sight of Billy Belchem's doelike eyes? Why didn't he just start his hair on fire and dance a jig while he went up in flames? It couldn't be any less shocking.

"I discovered that our impertinent Billy Smith is really the equally impertinent Billy Belchem," Fletcher said at last, knowing he had to say something. "He's a runaway, with a sermon-reading aunt in Tunbridge Wells. I'd like you to arrange to have him transported there posthaste, if you would."

Beck looked at his friend, unable to identify the tone of his voice. Fletcher sounded weary. Yes, that was it, weary, and somehow troubled. "Well, then," he said, forcing a smile, "it would seem you accomplished what you set out to do. That was what you set out to do, wasn't it, Fletcher? Get the boy alone and gain his confidence so that you could worm the truth out of him? You may have fooled your aunt, but then it doesn't take much subtlety to do that. I convinced myself you were only trying to do a good deed. Please accept my congratulations. What did it? Your open, honest face, or spending a few nights out of doors in the damp? I'd vote for your face, myself."

Fletcher smiled, his heart heavy as he remembered the spanking he had given Billy. Even Beck wouldn't consider that incident a good deed. "Thank you, Beck. Now, if you believe it possible, I should like to change the subject. I passed by the yellow saloon on my way upstairs. My compliments for a job well done. Has anything else transpired in my absence—not that I would think you had time for it."

Beck sat down, stretching his stiff leg out in front of him. "There was one thing, Fletch," he said, reaching into his pocket and extracting a worn, wrinkled envelope. "If you'll recall, you had your campaign bags sent directly on to Lakeview when you returned from Spain. I found them in the attics while I searched out the tables your aunt had ordered removed there from the yellow saloon, and took the liberty of unpacking them."

Fletcher gave a short laugh. "My campaign bags? That's a lovely way of speaking about the rags and tatters I brought back with me. You shouldn't have bothered, Beck. It would have been easier just to make a bonfire of the stuff, as I don't think I'm the sort of fellow to wax nostalgic over worn-out boots and faded uniforms."

Beck nodded his agreement. "That's precisely what I did with the majority of the stuff, saving only your shaving kit, as it came to you from your father, and a few other items." He held out the envelope. "They're packed away again in the attics. But I did think you might like to see this. I found it stuck in the lining of the smaller bag."

Fletcher rose to accept the envelope, taking hold of it gingerly. "I don't remember any envelope." He brought the thing closer to see that there was some inscription on it, half-hidden beneath smudges of dirt. "It's addressed to me and marked Personal," he said, walking over to his dresser to pick up a knife, breaking the seal.

Pulling out the single page that made up its contents, Fletcher allowed the envelope to fall to the floor as he unfolded the paper and exclaimed, "Good God, Beck, it's from William Darley. I've just been speaking of him with Billy. Now, why on earth do you suppose he would have written a letter to me, and then hidden it in my campaign bag?"

"Darley?" Beck repeated thoughtfully, moving closer, trying to read the letter over Fletcher's shoulder. "Isn't he the fellow you told me about, the one that saved your hide from some French sniper? What does it say?"

Fletcher stepped away from Beck, his voice shaking slightly as he read the words from his dead comrade-in-arms: " 'It would be a damn pity if you ever got to read this, my friend, for it would mean that my premonition has come true, and I am no longer with you. I can only hope I took a few dozen Old Trousers with me before I went. I had a dream last night, Fletch, a particularly nasty dream, in which I saw myself lying on the field of battle, my eyes open but not seeing anything, and a bloody great hole in my chest. It wasn't a pretty picture, let me tell you, and didn't flatter me at all.' "

"He imagined his own death?" Beck broke in, reaching for the brandy decanter. "That's bloody gruesome."

Fletcher barely heard him, for he was still reading. "What in Hades," he exclaimed, his jaw dropping. "Beck, listen to this: 'I've been watching you, Fletch, and listening to you when you talk about Arabella. No matter what you say, you're a decent man, and I know you were a fine brother. That's why I want you to take care of my sister if anything happens to me. I know I never mentioned her to you, but after hearing about Arabella, I didn't want to open old wounds by talking about Rosalie. We don't have anyone else, Rosalie and I, unless you count Mrs. Beale, and I certainly don't. The thought of having her in charge of poor Rosalie remains a more terrifying nightmare than the one I've just described, and her son, Sawyer, is even worse. I couldn't let such a sad fate befall my dearest sister. She's a good little girl, delicately nurtured, and bright as a penny. You'll adore her, Fletch, you really will.' "

"Which probably means she is a terrible, runny-nosed brat who puts toads in her governess's bed," Beck put in, shaking his head.

Fletcher shot his friend a quelling look and continued. " 'I've already written to tell her of my decision to name you as her guardian, and also told her how much I trust you to come to our aid. I know you'll do what's best for her until she reaches her majority or you can settle her in a respectable marriage. There's plenty of money for a Season in London if Rosalie wants one. This letter should serve to make it all legal with the solicitors, as I've had Captain Peterson witness it. Besides, with any luck at all, I'll tear this miserableness up tomorrow evening after the battle, and you'll never even see it.' "

Beck subsided into a chair as Fletcher refolded the letter and moved to stare out the window. "My God, Fletch, how long has William Darley been dead?"

"Months," Fletcher answered hollowly, noticing that his hands had begun to shake. "Months and months. Peterson died that day as well, which explains why he didn't come to me about the letter. My God, Beck, that poor little girl! What was her name? Rosalie? What can she be thinking?"

Beck leaned back, pursed his lips, and considered the question. "I would imagine," he said after a moment, "she is thinking that you, as well as her brother, are dead. Either that, or that you're the biggest rotter ever to draw breath."

Aunt Belleville, belatedly smarting ever so slightly under the niggling thought that her dearest nephew had only been flattering her and really did prefer the yellow saloon to be yellow, deliberately shunned the saloon and sat in the music room, her mind still struggling over the possibility of gilding the room's depressingly plain, domed ceiling.

Even Lethbridge, the dear man, had warned her that the price of gilt being what it was could put a crimp in her latest inspiration, giving rise to the unhappy thought that even dearest Lethbridge had attempted to tell her something. Perhaps, just perhaps, her contributions to the beautification of Lakeview were not appreciated.

"No, no, I must be wrong," she assured herself aloud, arranging her many-tasseled paisley scarf more comfortably about her shoulders. "My personal taste cannot be at fault, for surely I have been complimented on my dress more than once by the good women in the village. Perhaps there exists the problem of cost, although I have yet to see any hint of economizing in the way of cheaper vegetables or tallow candles."

The notion that her wonderful nephew could be penny-pinched brought a frown to Mrs. Belleville's round face. If economies must be employed, her days at Lakeview were numbered, for surely the first thing to go would be a useless female relative.

Aunt Belleville took her bottom lip between her teeth, pondering the distasteful thought of being once more set out upon the road, searching for some infirm relative to nurse in order to keep a roof over her own head.

She sighed, not for the first time repenting her decision to naysay Richard Casterbridge's proposal some forty years earlier. True, he had been a widower with six truly terrible children, a drafty old pile of a house somewhere near Newcastle, terrible teeth and worse breath, but he had offered her his hand in marriage, which was more than she could say about any other man she'd ever met. Besides, by now Richard's children would have been raised and, with any luck, Richard himself safely underground, and a drafty old pile of a house could be very comforting if it were her drafty old pile.

Aunt Belleville sat up very straight, resolving to spend no more precious time regretting past mistakes, and determined to think her way past her current problem. Clearly Lethbridge, who could not seem to take a hint even if it were dressed up in ribbons and placed in his porridge, was not about to rescue her through marriage—not that marriage to a butler was exactly what she had dreamed of when she turned down Richard. But Lethbridge was a lovely man and she silently acknowledged that she had grown a little long in the tooth to be picky.

No, she would have to discover some other way, some wondrously foolproof plan, to make herself indispensable to her nephew once more, and she had better locate it quickly, before the cook took to serving day-old bread or else she was apt to be the next "economy" at Lakeview.

Lethbridge had told her earlier that Fletcher had returned from his juvenile adventure of riding up and down the hills of the district, and none the happier than when he had gone, dragging that poor, hapless groom behind him, and was even now closeted upstairs with Beck, most probably going over the household accounts or some other troubling matter.

Had the beef been somewhat stringy at last night's supper, or was she worrying overmuch? Stringy beef, deep frowns over the purchase of a few small tables and some paint for the yellow saloon—was it that far a leap to seeing herself packing her bags so that there would be one less mouth to feed at Lakeview?

"Dear Aunt, I have run you to ground at last. I searched high and low for you in the yellow saloon and in the morning room, but it had not occurred to me that you might be hiding out in here. Have you by chance taken up the harp? What, ho! Can that be a frown I see on your sweet face? Don't tell me no one is dying, leaving you with nothing to do. How terribly inconsiderate. Should I summon up a cough, do you think, just to brighten your day?"

Aunt Belleville, startled, looked up to see her nephew standing in the doorway, looking so disgustedly healthy—not to mention handsome—that she found herself uncharacteristically longing to smack him in the face. If he loved her, had a smidgen of affection for her, he could at least be limping.

Fletcher abandoned his pose at the doorway to saunter into the room, gingerly seating himself in his late father's Sheraton wing chair, which had always been his favorite seat in the otherwise uncomfortably furnished room. His mother had been of the firm opinion that comfortable chairs in a music room were nothing more than an open invitation to impolite audiences to doze off during amateur performances. The Sheraton wing chair was her one concession to comfort, for it was either that, she knew, or evermore forgo her husband's presence in the room.

"Aunt Belleville," Fletcher began, wondering why he bothered to ask, but knowing he was a desperate man, "were there perhaps any communications delivered to Lakeview in my absence? Any, um, personal communications?''

His aunt seemed at a loss to understand him, which was clearly evident by her quizzical look. ''I should think Beck to be in charge of your communications, Fletcher. Besides, you were only gone from Lakeview for a few days. Were you expecting an important letter? Perhaps good news of a fortunate investment in the Exchange? Is a celebration in order? I could have the cook prepare a special dinner, which would be so much better than the stringy beef you missed at last night's meal.''

Fletcher looked at his aunt in bewilderment. He had never known the woman to be interested in financial affairs. ''No, no,'' he corrected, shaking his head. ''I've already questioned Beck about the last few days. I am thinking more of the months between Beck's departure for London and my return to Lakeview. Were there any letters, any communications, any visitors, I should be aware of?''

Aunt Belleville leaned forward anxiously. ''Are you in some sort of trouble, Fletcher? You haven't been gambling, have you? Gambling can be the very devil, you know. That's how my father lost his fortune, rest his soul, owing all to the cent-percenters in the end. I have a small sum set aside, if you should need it, although, of course, I shouldn't then be able to set out on my own, should I, and would have to remain here indefinitely.''

Fletcher put a hand to his mouth, considering his aunt's words. Clearly she was disturbed about something, and just as clearly the two of them were speaking at cross purposes. ''Am I in debt, Aunt?'' he asked at last. "I hadn't thought so, but you seem to believe I shall soon have dunners knocking down my door. Please enlighten me."

"You're not in debt?"

"On the contrary, Aunt. I am, if my solicitors and bankers are to be believed, quite disgustingly wealthy. Though I do thank you for the offer of a loan."

The woman's smile seemed to light up the room, then dimmed just as quickly. "Then you truly don't like my taste, and dearest Lethbridge was just saying that about the gilt in order not to hurt my feelings. I'm so ashamed."

"Guilt? Ashamed? What in Hades does guilt have to do with anything?" Fletcher considered this last outburst for a moment, then wisely decided to leave it alone when his aunt didn't answer, returning to the objective that had sent him searching for the woman in the first place.

"Were there any letters, or visitors, Aunt—any events out of the ordinary, that is—at Lakeview in the past few months?"

Aunt Belleville, brought back to attention by the rather strained tone of her nephew's question, put aside her own fears to concentrate on the problem at hand. Had there been any visitors, any communications out of the ordinary? She shook her head, dislodging several hairpins, then held up one finger as if that single digit had landed on just the thing.

"There was one very odd letter, as I recall, but it amounted to nothing in the end, because I didn't have the faintest idea what it meant. I answered it myself, not believing it necessary to bother Beck about it in London."

Now it was Fletcher's turn to lean forward in his seat. "Odd, Aunt? In what way?"

Aunt Belleville preened a moment, always happiest when she could be of service. "It was addressed very oddly, for one thing—to the house, rather than to anyone in particular—and the spelling and penmanship were truly atrocious. But I felt terribly sorry for the poor dear, for I am convinced I should certainly have perished in a fit if I should ever be put in her position, and answered her anyway."

Fletcher felt his head beginning to spin even as a cold dread invaded his stomach. "This letter, Aunt, was it perhaps from someone named Rosalie?"

"Rosalie?" his aunt answered slowly. "No, I can't say as it was."

Her nephew sat back dejectedly and his aunt's heart went out to him. "But it was about her," she added, hoping to be of some help. "Poor little soul. From what I could gather from the letter, it would seem she's gone missing."

"Missing?" Fletcher was on his feet in an instant. "Fetch me the letter immediately," he commanded rather harshly, unable to continue urging the information out of his aunt's muddled mind piece by maddening piece.

"If only I can find it!" Aunt Belleville rose, her paisley shawl falling to the floor as she raced from the room, a woman with a mission, to brush past a bewildered Lethbridge. "It is of the gravest import. My nephew must have the thing at once."

Lethbridge watched as the woman sailed down the hallway before entering the music room to glare at his employer. "If I might brook a suggestion, sir," the butler said, "I believe the lady to be overly concerned with pleasing you. Perhaps a little restraint in requesting favors from her would be in order, sir."

"I didn't ask her to leap from the roof with a rose between her teeth, Lethbridge," Fletcher responded dryly, taking in his butler's stern, condemning posture. "But I will in future, on your suggestion, be more prudent in phrasing my requests."

Lethbridge bowed from the waist, his bones creaking audibly with the effort, and withdrew, leaving Fletcher once more to ponder the advisability of gifting his aunt with a dowry, holding a gun to his butler's head until a marriage ceremony could be performed, and then personally sending them both to China for a prolonged wedding trip.

A few moments later his aunt returned, breathing heavily from her exertion on his behalf and waving a piece of paper in front of her like a fan. "I've found it, Fletcher. It wasn't with my knitting, which is odd, for I usually keep important papers with my knitting, but it was in my desk drawer, of all places, right next to my watercolor of that lovely abbey I visited so many years ago."

She continued to fan herself with the letter as Fletcher made two fruitless grabs for it, continuing, "I don't remember the exact name of the abbey. Of course, it is no more than ruins and not a real abbey at all anymore. It was named after some popish saint, I believe. Fletcher, is there a Saint Walter? No, that couldn't be it."

"Aunt, if you please?" His teeth clenched, Fletcher made one last, desperate grab for the letter. The next thing he knew, he held the bottom half of the letter, with the remainder of the thing still firmly clutched in his aunt's trembling paw. "Oh, good grief!"

Aunt Belleville looked at the scrap of paper in her hand, then at Fletcher. "Do you feel all right, my dear?" she asked, unable to fathom his urgency over a communication that, besides being worthless, was more than six weeks old. "Perhaps you could do with a dose of that lovely medicine I picked up from the village herbalist last week. Mrs. Eton swears by it, although she does use it for her monthly miseries, but I'm sure it has other uses."

Fletcher had gone beyond seeing the humor in the situation. He had failed William Darley, failed his friend, who had saved his life. How could he not have seen the letter in his campaign bag? How could he have stayed in London, trailing from party to party, and sent those same bags to Lakeview without looking in them? How could he live another moment without knowing what this mysterious communication would tell him about William Darley's orphaned sister?

He snatched the remainder of the letter from his aunt's hand and went over to the pianoforte to piece the two ragged halves together. His shoulders slumped visibly as he read, his worst fears confirmed the moment he saw the signature of Mrs. Beale, the woman William had mentioned as being a totally unsuitable guardian for young Rosalie.

Reading the letter proved worse than hearing that it existed, for Mrs. Beale had written to tell him that Rosalie, "bringing shame and mortification upon us all," had run away from home.

"A rather overvolatile child," Rosalie had refused to behave as she ought, wearing black and working a remembrance sampler in her brother's honor—and had chosen instead to weave fanciful lies about one Fletcher Belden, who, like some knight on a white stallion, would be coming to rescue her from her aunt. "As if dearest William would have entrusted his sister to anyone save her adoring aunt."

The letter concluded with the fervent wish that Rosalie, "overwrought and prone to fanciful exaggeration of mind," had indeed bolted for Lakeview and would now, upon receipt of this missive, be returned posthaste to the bosom of her family.

"And she mentions something about offering a reward, just to make it worth my while," Fletcher said aloud, pushing the pieces of paper into his breast pocket in disgust.

"Yes," Aunt Belleville said from behind him, "I too thought that last bit distasteful, although I do feel for the woman. After all, the child has run away. There is no end to the trouble a young female could tumble into alone on the road. I wrote back, of course, telling Mrs. Beale that I could not help her as no Rosalie had ever appeared at Lakeview, and that constituted the end of it. Tell me, Fletcher, how did you come to hear about this Rosalie person?"

But Fletcher wasn't listening. He was already halfway to the door, bellowing for Beck at the top of his lungs and leaving his aunt curiously comforted. Clearly she was to remain at Lakeview, if only to lend comfort to her poor, brain-addled nephew.

It was a few minutes past midnight, and Billy had been abed in the last stall on the left since ten, having packed her meager belongings shortly after dinner in preparation of her planned departure from Lakeview before dawn the next morning.

She slept, but only fitfully, her mind filled with a variety of thoughts, each more depressing than the last—many of them having to do with the reluctance she felt at the idea of passing out of Fletcher Belden's life forever—so that if someone were to look closely, it would be easy to see the tracks where a few tears had dried on her face.

Because her sleep was so disturbed, or possibly because the nocturnal intruder proved so clumsy as to overturn a large oak bucket near the stable door, Billy was more than half-awake to hear a mournful male voice groan out, "Rosalie, Rosalie, wherefore art thou, Rosalie?"

Her blood running cold, Billy sat up, clutching a thin woolen blanket against her chest. "Who—who's out there?"

A moment later Fletcher Belden's golden head appeared around the edge of the stall, his hair falling boyishly onto his forehead, his usually clear eyes bleary with drink, and his normally perfectly groomed body wearing naught but boots, breeches, and a white, flowing, half-undone shirt. He looked, in a word, wonderful, and Billy longed to hate him. "It's the evil guardian, Billy-boy. Who did you think it was, Father Christmas?"

Billy mastered the urge to rise up and take Fletcher's sagging body into her arms, offering comfort to his obviously tortured soul, but chose instead to concentrate on the decanter of brandy in his hand and the odor of strong spirits on his breath.

"You're drunk," she pointed out unnecessarily as

Fletcher, still retaining his death grip on the wall of the stall, was at that moment sliding slowly to his knees in the straw.

"Drunk? Me?" Fletcher returned haughtily, lifting his head to attempt focusing his eyes on Billy. "How dare you, sirrah! I am not drunk. I'm fat is a faddle."

"That's fit as a fiddle, sir," Billy corrected sadly, unable to resist reaching out to help the man into a more comfortable position, his back leaning against the stable wall, his long legs splayed out in front of him.

His head lolling on his neck, Fletcher grinned impishly in Billy's direction. "Isn't that what I said? Never mind, it doesn't matter. What are you doing here, Billy?"

"I sleep here, if you'll recall," she informed him, prudently prying the crystal decanter out of Fletcher's nerveless fingers before sitting down beside him. "The question remains, however, as to what you are doing here. If you've come to cast up your accounts safely away from your precious carpets, I would much rather you didn't. It smells horrid enough in here as it is."

Fletcher laid his head against Billy's shoulder, nearly toppling her. "No, no, that's not why I came," he said quietly. "I did have a reason, though, I'm sure of that. You make a nice pillow, Billy, do you know that? Of course you know that. You're very soft for a lad, very, very soft."

Billy's heart leapt in her chest at his words, and she pushed at Fletcher until he was sitting upright once more. "I'll go fetch Hedge and we'll take you back to the house," she said, trying to rise.

Fletcher's right hand snaked out to rudely push her back down. "Don't leave me, Billy," he seemed to all but plead. "I promise you, I won't disgrace myself. That was the brandy talking, but I'm all right now. And I even remember why I came. I want to apologize to you for that spanking. It was wrong; I was wrong. I'm not your guardian. I'm not a fit person to be anyone's guardian."

"Who—who wants you to be a guardian?" Billy asked, remembering with foreboding what Fletcher had said when he first entered the stables.

Spreading his arms wide, Fletcher exclaimed, "Who doesn't? First my father entrusts my darling Arabella into my care. Then Christine Denham uses me as a guardian angel to bring her beloved to his senses. Not content with that, I deliberately set out to act as guardian—nay, Good Samaritan—to a young gentleman out on his own. That's you, of course," he interjected, giving Billy's soft belly a sharp poke. "But now, now, I've got the worst of it—the very worst of it—thanks to William Darley."

Billy barely restrained an overpowering urge to burst into tears. "William Darley? Isn't that the soldier friend you talked about last night? The man who died?"

Fletcher nodded, reaching for the decanter. "He left me his sister, Rosalie. Lovely name, isn't it? Rosalie Darley. A person could write poems to a Rosalie Darley, if a person could write poems. I can't, not even here, in the Lake District, where everyone and his brother writes poems. William's baby sister. But I didn't know. I never looked. And now she has run away—to God knows where—and all because I didn't know. I didn't look. Just like Arabella." He pushed back his head to look sightlessly at the ceiling. "Wherefore art thou, Rosalie?" he asked the broad, bare boards.

Billy knew what Fletcher referred to, and her heart ached for him. She had heard the stories of Arabella, his young sister, and how she had fallen in love with a French prisoner, gotten with child, and committed suicide rather than tell her brother of her shame. Clearly Fletcher blamed himself, although, to Billy's mind, he couldn't have known what his sister had been doing.

After all, it wasn't as if she had been entertaining her Frenchman in the house. Besides, there existed no being sneakier than a woman—wasn't she proof of that? No mere man could possibly feel responsible for anything a woman set her mind to do—not if that woman wanted to hide it from him.

Christine Denham remained a puzzle, however. Billy had heard the name, or at least she thought she had, yet it rang no warning bells in her head. But Fletcher's last bout of guardianship—his attempt to set his groom's feet back on the straight-and-narrow—had certainly been fraught with problems, and for that Billy knew she could take full blame.

Fletcher's head began to droop toward her shoulder once more, and this time Billy allowed it. "Do you mean to say that you didn't know William Darley left guardianship of his sister—Rosalie, I believe you said—to you? How did you find out?"

"The letter," Fletcher slurred against her shoulder. "Beck found the letter. Two letters. Mrs. Beale wrote the second one. Terrible woman, offering a reward. Very low-minded. But Rosalie's gone. I've failed again."

Billy bit on her knuckle, trying to think, even while she was silently rejoicing that Fletcher had never meant to let William down. Could it work? Could she possibly fool him? "Maybe—maybe she'll turn up, now that you're back at Lakeview," she put in hopefully, a plan forming in her mind. "After all, it is some distance from Patterdale to here, isn't it, at least for a young girl traveling alone? Perhaps this Rosalie stopped along the way, to work for her supper, and will arrive anytime now."

"Perhaps. I can't spare time to take you to Tunbridge Wells now, you understand," Fletcher said abruptly, as if suddenly remembering his mission to the stables. "I planned to have Beck send you on the stagecoach, but that would be too easy for me, and another blotch on my copybook as far as acting the good guardian, wouldn't it?"

"I wouldn't mind, sir, really I wouldn't," Billy interrupted quickly, feeling very sorry for Fletcher—even more sorry for him, in fact, than she felt for herself, and Billy felt extremely sorry for herself indeed.

"No, I must first find Rosalie. Only then will I be able to return you to your aunt. But you must come live at the house. No more sleeping in the stables. You've been punished enough. Come on now," he urged, struggling to get to his feet while holding on to Billy's sleeve. "It's late, and little boys should be tucked up in their beds. Besides, I've already lost Rosalie. Can't be mislaying you as well, can I?"

Billy opened her mouth to protest just as Beck stepped into the stall to grab hold of Fletcher's arm. "I'll take him," he said, motioning Billy back. "And if you're as wise as I believe you to be, you'll forget Mr. Belden's visit this evening. He has had a rather trying day and cannot be held responsible. Do we understand each other, young man?"

"Completely," Billy answered, more grateful than angry at Beck's interruption. She bent down to take up the decanter and held it out to him. "And I haven't seen this either."

Fletcher, who had been rubbing at his eyes, seemed to sober momentarily. "Beck, my good friend, have you come to scold me or to take me to bed? I'd much prefer the bed, actually, as I don't think I feel very well." He grabbed hold of Beck's shirt front. "You won't tell Aunt Belleville, will you? She'll give me something awful to drink, and a sermon as well."

"It will be our secret, Fletch," Beck promised, leading his friend away as Billy slowly subsided into a pile of straw, wondering how in the world she could keep her secret once she found herself installed in one of Lakeview's bedrooms. Eyeing the small pack of her belongings, she entertained and just as quickly dismissed the idea of running away.

She had run away enough. The time had come to stand and face the consequences of her actions—especially now, while Fletcher felt so guilty about "poor Rosalie." He might, she tried to console herself, even let me live once the truth comes out.

Fletcher woke from a troubled sleep just as the clock in the foyer struck out the hour of six, a look of pure astonishment on his face, as he had finally succeeded in putting a name to his niggling suspicion. Weary as he was, drunk as he was, something was bothering him—something Billy had said.

He scrambled out of bed in the near dark, his head pounding, his tongue feeling twice its size, to grope on his desktop for the pieces of Mrs. Beale's letter, before wasting more precious minutes as his uncooperative fingers worked the tinderbox trying to light his bedside candle.

Squeezing his eyes nearly shut in order to focus on the words, he looked beneath Mrs. Beale's signature for her address, and his heart skipped a beat.

And there it was. Damn all lying, conniving, modest, soft, infuriating grooms to the gates of hell and beyond—there it was!

" 'After all, it is some distance from Patterdale to here, isn't it, at least for a young girl traveling alone?' " he recited in a singsong voice, repeating Billy Belchem's words as he looked down at Mrs. Beale's nearly unintelligible handwriting and the words "Hilltop Farm, Patterdale."

"Perverse, am I? Gently nurtured child, is she? How could I have been so blind?" In a bellow that had Beck all but tumbling out of bed to run down the hall to his friend, Fletcher raised his fist and vowed, "I'll murder the brat!"

7

The morning dawned brightly, as if purposely to mock Rosalie's dark-gray mood of flat despair, and Hedge arrived soon after, bursting from the tack room with a spring to his step and a lilt in his voice—a sure sign that he had already been at his store of brandy—warning Rosalie that she was very definitely in for a long day.

"Pry dem peepers open, yer lazy slug," Hedge ordered, giving Rosalie's leg a painful kick as she curled herself into a fetal position on the mound of straw and did her best to feign slumber. "Yer gots animals ter tend."

Rosalie groaned, sitting up to grab at her abused shin. "Just brimming over with the milk of human kindness again, aren't you, Hedge?" she grumbled at his retreating back, although careful to keep her voice low so that the man couldn't hear her.

Sighing deeply, she stood up, folded her thin blanket, and ran a hand through her hair.

She'd kill for a bath, Rosalie acknowledged silently, reaching for a clean piece of straw to gnaw on in the hope it would sweeten her breath.

She'd give up her hope of salvation for a night between real sheets, in a real bed.

She'd climb any mountain for a pair of soft leather

slippers to replace the heavy boots that had raised hard calluses on her heels; swim any river to sit at table and have someone pass her fresh hot bread and jelly.

"I want to be Rosalie again," she wailed, her nearly sleepless night and the all but overwhelming burden of her problems loosening her tongue at precisely the wrong moment.

Hedge's head popped around the edge of the stall. His jug ears seemed to quiver as if caught in a high wind. His bloodshot, dirt-brown eyes nearly bulged out of his head. "Wot did yer say?" he questioned in his most piercing voice. "Yer wants ter be who agin?"

Rosalie would have kicked herself if she believed the feat to be humanly possible. As it wasn't, and she had no intention of offering the job of rump-kicker to Hedge, she took refuge in bluster.

"What nonsense can you be talking about? I didn't say anything," she railed in a challenging tone. "Do you drink 'round the clock now, Hedge, instead of just morning till night? Don't tell me you've taken to hearing strange voices now." She shook her head, a deliberately woeful look on her face. "Tsk, tsk. Bad sign, that."

But Hedge, who'd had just enough brandy to sharpen his wits, rather than to dull them, wasn't about to be taken in by Rosalie's attempt at deflection. Striding into the stall on his bandy legs, his hands clamped on his hips, he pushed his head forward on his skinny neck and looked intently into Rosalie's eyes.

A long moment later he turned his head to one side and spit with great accuracy, hitting a horsefly in midflight and knocking it, buzzing angrily, to the straw. "Yer are! Yer a bloody chick-a-biddy," he accused, glaring at Rosalie once again. "Rosalie, huh? Well, if that don't beat the Dutch!"

A sick dread invaded Rosalie's stomach as her knees began to knock together in fright. "You—you're not going to cry beef on me, Hedge?"

Hedge's head snapped backward. "Me? Would yer be daft, gel? An' 'ow would it look—me bein' taken in by a snip of a gel? Yer bubbled me good, yer did, an' Oi'm not about ter make m'self a laughin'stock outta me own mouth."

Rosalie would have fallen on the man's neck in gratitude, if only Hedge were even slightly more prudent in his bathing habits. She restrained herself, saying only, "You have my thanks, Hedge, and I will work twice as hard as before, just to make it up to you. You are indeed the best of good fellows."

Hedge sniffed, grumbling something about having Rosalie do twice the work she'd done before would be a welcome change from the work she was doing now, which wasn't worth a rat's rump anyway, before asking, "Wot wuz yer doin' on the road anyways, Rosie? Summone atter yer?"

Was someone after her? Rosalie considered this for a moment. Yes, that sounded fairly good, and by the look on Hedge's face, he would very much like to hear an interesting story. Far be it from her to disoblige the man!

"As a matter of fact, Hedge, I am running away from—from, um, the workhouse, where my mean uncle had put me when he took our land. My mother was there with me, but she died, of a broken heart most likely. And the master . . . Well, let's just say he was beginning to look at me with a strange gleam in his beady little eyes. I knew I had to get away. I knew something about horses, as I always rode at home before my father died and evil Uncle Arnold took everything from us, and so I came here."

Now, Hedge was not known to be the sharpest shaft in the quiver at the best of times, and he hadn't seen the best of times in a score of brandy-soaked years, so it cannot be too difficult to understand that Rosalie's story—a hastily spun, flimsy tissue of outlandish lies—was still strong enough to bind the muck-loving Hedge to her side.

"Yer poor, bleedin' lamb," the ex-jockey lamented, cuffing her affectionately on the shoulder, proving to Rosalie that the man could as easily swallow a bag of moonshine as he could a flagon of ale. "But we cain't let the master 'ear, fer if 'e was ter rumble yer lay, it could be curtains fer the two of us. So no more talkin' ter yerself about bein' a gel, yer 'ear? Jist keep yer chaffer close an' Oi promises not ter cry rope on yer."

Rubbing her shoulder, Rosalie vigorously nodded her agreement, knowing that Hedge was more concerned for his own position than he was for hers, but she was not about to take him to task about his want of chivalry. "You're too kind, Hedge. And I promise, just as soon as I can, I will leave Lakeview, just so that Mr. Belden never learns that you've been keeping an innocent young girl in the stables."

"Innocent young gel . . ." Hedge repeated, rubbing reflectively at the stubble on his chin as the full import of Rosalie's words struck him. "Yer better would," he ordered, stepping back a pace, as if to distance himself from her. "But fer now, the geldin's gone an' spavined, an' needs some 'ot fomentations right smart.

The leg'll blow up like a bladder fer a bit, but soon be fine—iffen yer do it right. Can yer 'andle that, Rosie?''

Taking her cue from Hedge, Rosalie nodded, adding only, ''That I can, Hedge, just as long as you promise to stop calling me Rosie.''

Hedge spat, this time missing a sitting spider by nearly a full inch, and cursed under his breath. Without another word, he turned and headed for the tack room, from where Rosalie was certain he would not stir for the remainder of the day, which was a very good thing, for she had a lot of thinking to do.

Taking only enough time to quickly splash her face with cold water and rinse her mouth, she began working her way down the length of the double-sided stables: she fed and watered the horses, shoveled out the evidence of those same horses' efficient digestive systems, turned several of the mounts out into the fenced pasture, and put a poultice on the gelding's leg. Then she took up a brush and began to curry Pagan's silken ebony flanks.

All the while Rosalie worked, she thought about her ever-growing problem.

She did not spend too much time considering whatever character flaw she must possess that had her continually falling into scrapes, for she had been involved in one scrape or another ever since she could remember, most of them, according to William, caused by her overactive imagination.

She did spare a moment to congratulate herself for the highly inspired crammer she had recently spoon-fed to Hedge, for she had somehow unerringly found the single soft spot the man possessed—a fine sense of self-preservation—as well as one of his many weaknesses—the love of a story that smacked of juicy scandal.

What she did concentrate on was the pursuit of some way out of her current predicament, a maddening jumble caused by her nocturnal departure from Hilltop Farms, her masquerade as a groom, her lies—(all of them)—Fletcher's ill-timed belated discovery that he had been named her guardian, his plan to install her in his house until shipping her off to her "aunt" in Tunbridge Wells, and—this most of all—her growing feelings for the man.

Her first impulse had had a lot to do with her skulking away into the night after having appropriated the gold sugar sifter she had espied one day when sent to the kitchens for a piece of raw meat to soothe Hedge's black eye, an injury received by way of his rude introduction to the bottom half of the top half of a divided door. She would replace the sifter, naturally, once she had been hailed on the London stage as the most acclaimed actress in a decade, and then, her conscience clear, she would feel free to become Prinny's mistress.

That plan had gone swiftly by the boards the moment Fletcher had staggered into the stables, calling out her true name. Her heart had fairly broken for him as he related his sad tale, and she could no more add to his feelings of inadequacy as a fit guardian than drive a stake through his tender heart.

She had almost blurted out the truth then and there, even if he had been too drunk to realize what she was saying, but was forestalled when he told her she would have to move into the house. Immediately she had realized that the very last thing she wanted was Fletcher to ever know that she had first presented herself to him as a groom.

Oh, she could have done it if there were nothing between the two of them but a few words spoken in passing between employer and hired servant. But they had shared much more than that—considerably more—including, she thought, blushing, a bed.

It was impossible for her to simply stand up and say, "Surprise! Your search has ended, Fletcher, and by the by, you aren't really in danger of becoming perverted. I am a woman of eighteen, not a boy. Not only that, but I am Rosalie, your missing ward. Oh, yes, and one thing more: I think I am falling in love with you. Isn't that above everything wonderful?"

Wonderful? Hardly. He would blink once or twice, his mouth dropping open. He would rejoice in the knowledge that William Darley's sister had been found.

For a moment.

And then, remembering their night at the inn, recalling the intimacy they had shared and the fool he had made of himself trying to impress her with his manliness, he would kill her. Love? The last thing Fletcher Belden would ever feel for Rosalie Darley was love.

No, she thought, running the brush down Pagan's quivering shank, she must find some way to leave Lakeview, and she must leave today.

She decided her first step would be to return to the place where she had buried her bag containing, among other things, her gown, undergarments, shoes, and cape. She wished she could remember if the spot was exactly two or three trees to the north of the stone that looked like a sheep's head. She would bathe in some secluded beck, dress herself, and then present her person to Lakeview as the long-lost Rosalie Elizabeth Darley.

No one would recognize her as being Billy Belcham, or at least she fervently prayed they would not. People saw what they expected to see—everybody knew that. They had seen a small, slim lad with a dirty face. There was no reason for anyone to look deeper.

"Except for Fletcher," she reminded herself, walking around to attack Pagan's ebony coat from the other side.

Be that as it may be, she decided, no one would look at a well-scrubbed Rosalie Darley and see Billy Belchem—not even Fletcher—especially since there was no possible way anyone could stand the two of them side by side and make comparisons.

She worried at her lower lip with her teeth, doing her utmost to convince herself that at last she had hit on a plan that would work, so lost in a brown study as she bent to smooth Pagan's foreleg that she did not hear Fletcher approaching along the center aisle that ran down the stable.

He stopped a scant five feet away, to rake her with his eyes, eyes that, now that the scales had been stripped away from them, took in every betraying curve that proclaimed that Billy Belchem was indeed a female.

How he had been so blind he could not fathom, for her every graceful, feminine movement screamed her sex to any who took the time to really look at her. It was no wonder she had intrigued him from the moment he'd first laid eyes on her; it was no wonder he had been drawn to her.

What was a wonder was that he had needed to be hit over the head with a red brick to figure it out.

Fletcher moved a step closer, remembering how he

had felt upon awakening at the inn, as if he had held something precious in his arms, only to let it slip away. Fast upon that memory came the shame of knowing that he had slept in the buff. No wonder Billy—no, Rosalie—had been looking at him so strangely from her perch on the window seat. By rights the girl should have been dissolved in strong hysterics.

By rights, the girl should be locked in a bedroom on a ration of stale bread and brackish water! By rights, the girl should be read a lecture on behavior befitting a female until her ears burned a bright red! By rights, the girl—who was, contrary to his and Beck's first thoughts, most definitely not a young child still putting frogs in her governess's bed—should be married!

Married? Fletcher staggered beneath this new, damning thought. He had been so angry, so self-directed in his thoughts ever since realizing that Billy Belcham was Rosalie Darley, that it had taken him this long to come to the conclusion that should have smacked him square in the face the moment he'd discovered her true identity.

He, Fletcher Belden, carefree bachelor and a man who had promised himself that the one thing he needed was a prolonged break from female companionship, had taken up with a young woman within minutes of his return to Lakeview, carted that same young woman all over the Lake District, inherited her as his ward, and was, after compromising her in nearly every way possible, now honor-bound to marry her.

"Talk about being punished for your sins," he murmured disgustedly. "I hadn't known I have lived such a terrible life that this should be my fate." And then, surprising himself, Fletcher smiled.

"You! What are you about, sneaking up on a person like that?"

Fletcher, not realizing that he had spoken aloud, was startled by Rosalie's abrupt attack as well as by his strange delight at the thought of his impending marriage to her, and he responded the only way he could without resorting to actual physical violence.

Eyeing her from head to foot and back again, quietly taking in the distinct feminine cast of her features and the small, square hands that could have belonged to a lad but definitely did not, he pointed out coldly, "You're filthy, boy, and your hair looks like a birch broom in a fit. What do you do—comb it with a rake?"

Rosalie opened her mouth to speak, then thought better of it. How could she possibly have been feeling sorry for this insufferable man? What maggot had invaded her brain to have her believe she could actually love him?

She leaned against the side of the stall, the brush propped on her hip, and quipped, "How's your head, Mr. Belden, sir? Or would it be your stomach that delights in giving you the devil this morning? I must say, you don't look well."

Fletcher refused to take the bait and only smiled, his tanned skin crinkling around the outer corners of his eyes in a way that turned Rosalie's insides to melted butter.

"I feel wonderful, Billy, much more the thing, thank you for asking. It takes more than a little brandy to lay me by the heels, although I do apologize for disturbing your rest last night. I don't make a habit of drinking to excess, you know, although I am no Methodist either, and have been known to kick up a lark now and then.

I didn't bore you with any sad stories, did I? I can't seem to remember much of anything about most of the evening,'' he lied smoothly, as inspiration hit him, ''although Beck has taken great pains this morning to read me at least a partial listing of my sins.''

''You don't remember anything?'' Rosalie asked intently, her hopes already leaping for the boughs as she unwarily took Fletcher's bait. ''Nothing? Nothing at all?''

Little demon, Fletcher thought, watching in amusement as a spark of mischief invaded Rosalie's green eyes. He wondered yet again precisely how old she was. It was deuced difficult telling age with these small ones. She could be anything from seventeen to twenty. ''Barely a thing,'' he said when he thought he had made her hold her breath long enough in anticipation of his answer. ''Why, did I say something terrible?''

''No! No, not at all,'' Rosalie exclaimed quickly, her agile brain having lit on a solution to her problems. ''You told me you had only come to the stables to advise me of your plans to have Beck find me a seat on the stagecoach so that I can join my aunt in Tunbridge Wells as soon as possible. Poor lady. You convinced me that she must be completely distracted over my absence. Don't you remember?''

Fletcher shook his head, his expression blank, willing to play Rosalie's game a little longer, just to see where her devious brain would take them. ''No, I can't say that I do. I seem to have forgotten more than I remember.''

''Oh, that is too bad,'' Rosalie commiserated, coming out of Pagan's stall to pass by Fletcher on her way to check on the gelding, his unwavering gray stare beginning to wear on her already ragged nerves. "Then you also do not remember how I begged you not to put yourself out for me, as I have had enough of being a groom and, with the money I have set aside, had already decided to book passage on the coach leaving the village this afternoon."

The devil you will, Fletcher thought, still refusing to smile.

"I shall hate leaving Hedge in the lurch, what with all these animals to tend to, but you have made me see the grave error of my ways in running off as I did. I have responsibilities to shoulder, and am now ready to face them like a man. You were," she added prudently, her back still to Fletcher, "quite pleased with the arrangement, sir, as I remember it, and wished me godspeed."

"I didn't! But what of my plan to have you move into the house, just until I have located my ward? I did tell you I have a ward, didn't I?"

"Yes, indeed, sir, you did, which was just another reason I could not let you become a martyr in my cause," Rosalie improvised, turning to face him but as yet unable to meet his eyes. "You have enough on your plate now, kind sir, and although you have done me a signal honor by suggesting it, I am afraid I really must turn down your kind invitation."

Fletcher had to turn away to hide his grin. It was the "kind sir" that had done it. Oh, the business about it being a "signal honor" was delicious, but the "kind sir" had put the capper on it.

He'd say one thing for Rosalie Darley: she thought fast on her feet. If it weren't for her tendency to overact, she might still have him believing that she was in truth

Billy Belchem. Turning back to her, he said kindly, "It is you, dear Billy, who should not become a martyr in my cause."

"But—"

Fletcher raised a hand to forestall her protest. "I don't want to hear another word. Now, I know I was very drunk last night, as I could not otherwise have agreed to such a plan, and I now rescind my permission for you to leave. You will pack up your things and move into the house at once, where I can keep an eye on you until such time as I am free to personally escort you to Tunbridge Wells. A fine young lad like you forced out onto the road again, alone? No, no. I would not sleep nights, halfling."

"But, sir," Rosalie insisted, still doing her best to wriggle out of the noose she could feel fastening tight about her throat—so tightly, in fact, that she couldn't even draw enough breath to whistle her beetle-headed plan of running off and returning as herself down the wind. "I could not sponge on you. Please, if you won't let me go, at least allow me to stay here, in the stables, where I may be of some assistance to Hedge."

"Sponge on me?" Fletcher repeated, at last feeling as if he were beginning to get a little of his own back. "I seem to have misled you, halfling." His next words were couched in the terms of a demand. "You won't be sponging on me. Indeed, no. You shall be my personal servant for the time you remain at Lakeview. Remember how well you did with my boots? Beck labors morn till night, what with the two of us having been in London for so long, and I'm sure he will appreciate the relief your presence will bring. Now, drop that brush at once and come along."

Rosalie was willing to fight to the bitter end, but she

was also intelligent enough to know when the battle was over, and logical enough to know that she had lost. "Yes, sir, Mr. Belden, sir," she grumbled, flinging the brush to the floor before going to fetch her bundled belongings.

A few moments later, Fletcher in the lead—his long-legged strides forcing Rosalie to take two steps to his one—the two of them were on their way across the lawn to the house.

From his vantage point hidden behind the half-door to She-Devil's stall, Hedge, who had heard every word that had passed between his employer and the groom, reached inside his shirt for the flask he always kept close to his heart, suddenly in dire need of a restorative drink.

"Oh, gloomy hour," Hedge moaned in self-pity, wiping his mouth with the back of his hand. " 'E knows, Rosie, m'gel. Sure as check, Belden knows. Why'd yer hafta pick this 'ere stable ter light in? We're both in fer it now."

There were many things in life that Fletcher viewed with delight, among them being a fine meal, a good joke, the company of friends, and the smell of the morning after a spring rain. But there was nothing more certain to bring him pleasure than to watch his lifelong friend, Beck, at a loss for words.

Fletcher, having completed his disclosure of Rosalie's true identity—a revelation he had drawn out with considerable glee—sat back in his chair and allowed his heart to be filled with the satisfaction that Beck's unnaturally pale complexion and slack jaw engendered in him.

"He—he's a she?" Beck got out at last, still standing

so stiffly that he appeared for all intents and purposes as if he had been stuffed. "He—he's your she? I mean, she's Rosalie?"

Fletcher's smile carved a slashing dimple in his cheek. "How clever of you, Beck," he commented pleasantly. "Your statement, although barely coherent, actually seems to rhyme. Yes, my friend, my he's a she—she's Rosalie. Fairly boggles the mind, don't it? Not the rhyming—although the feat remains remarkable—but the success the brat has had with her devious little deception."

Beck was not amused. "Oh, shut up," he ordered distractedly, collapsing into a chair to glare at his employer. "You must still be castaway if you can find any humor in such a terrible situation. Only think, Fletch—you slept with the girl!"

"Hardly, Beck," Fletcher corrected, although his smile did slip a notch. "If I had truly slept with her, the deception wouldn't have lasted until her verbal slip last night. And I must remind you that you still haven't complimented me on my fine powers of detection, considering the fact that I was more than three parts drunk at the time."

"My congratulations," Beck bit out, knowing he would have no peace until he had actually uttered the words.

"Thank you, my friend. And now, to continue my rebuttal to your statement that I have slept with the young lady. My best guess would be that Rosalie is about nineteen years of age, hardly William's infant sister. I may not have your wide experience with women—devil that you are—but I've slept with enough of them to know that there exists a distinct anatomical difference between them and ourselves. I slept beside the girl, which is very different. And so, I repeat, our relationship was completely innocent."

"Innocent? Innocent!" Beck was on his feet once more, pacing stiff-leggedly up and down the length of Fletcher's bedchamber. At last he stopped, directly in front of his friend, and pointed an accusing finger. "With, beside—it makes no difference. Not to the world, anyway. You'll have to marry her. You do know that, don't you, Fletch?"

Fletcher closed his eyes, nodding. "I know that, Beck."

"Well, good," Beck responded weakly, surprised at Fletcher's ready acceptance of a fate he knew the man had vowed to avoid for as long as humanly possible. "I don't suppose you're pleased."

Fletcher grinned, not about to gift his friend with his innermost thoughts. Not this time, when his heart was involved as it had never been before, not even during his association with Christine Denham.

"Ah, Beck," he said silkily, "you know me so well. No, I am not pleased, not pleased at all. You know it, I know it, and when I am ready, our little groom will know it."

"When you're ready?" Beck felt his muscles clench as he watched Fletcher's expression. "Uh-oh, I know that look, and I can't say I like it one bit. You're up to no good, aren't you, Fletch?"

Rising, Fletcher deliberately donned a most innocent, injured expression—just the sort that would have had Aunt Belleville running for the syrup of figs if she had been gifted with the sight of it. "Me, Beck? Can you be insinuating that I am a mean, perhaps even petty person? Can you be saying that I am out to punish poor Rosalie Darley, merely because she rigged herself up in boy's clothing, passed herself off as a groom, allowed me to sleep beside her, naked as the day I was brought into this world, putting me through several levels of hell? Then she stood back and watched while I proceeded to make a complete cake of myself for feeling attracted to her, and trying to convince the both of us that I was more manly than Gentleman Jackson in his prime—if you laugh, Beck, by God, I'll have your heart on a spit—and all of this because she wanted to check up on me? Could you possibly also be saying that you believe a man—I?—would stoop so low as to wish to wreak revenge on such a maddening, trouble-causing infant as my ward?''

Beck was unmoved by this outburst, although the thought of Fletcher believing he had been attracted to a young boy was, in truth, rather amusing. Folding his hands across his chest, he responded dryly, ''Yes, Fletch. You.''

Fletcher's grin split his face. ''Ah, Beck, how well you know me. Of course I'm going to put her through a few hoops before telling her I know her true identity. I'd be ashamed of myself if I didn't.''

''Leaving it to me to feel ashamed for you,'' Beck groused resignedly, sitting once more. ''It will end badly, mark you. I can feel it in my bones, and I, for one, want nothing to do with it. Exactly what nefarious plan dances in your head? And why have you ordered that tub brought back in here? You already had a bath this morning.''

Fletcher shook his head. ''What a bundle of contradictions you harbor, Beck. You want nothing to do with it, yet you insist upon hearing all the details. Perhaps I won't tell you."

Beck wasn't dismayed. "And perhaps I shall march directly down the hall to Miss Rosalie Darley's bedchamber and inform her that we have become aware of her identity."

Fletcher inspected his shirt cuffs. "It remains remarkable, the sheer lack of terror I instill in the members of this household. As a matter of fact, except for the incidence of the elephant feet, Aunt Belleville seems to be my only solace, even going so far as to worry herself about the state of my finances. You, however, and Lethbridge, seem to believe you have been gifted with some God-given right to bully me at every turn."

"What are you planning?" Beck asked again, his lack of fear showing both his lifelong affection for Fletcher and his knowledge that the man was never truly malicious.

"I'll need three days, as I see it," Fletcher told him, watching as two footmen brought in pails of water for his bath. "It will take that long for Mrs. Beale, who I am sure will prove a most poisonous female, and Sawyer, whoever he might be, to join us here after my letter arrives at Hilltop Farm. One day to put Billy Belchem—Lord, how I hate that name; Belchem, Belden, just as if she'd planned it that way—firmly in his place for making a May game of me, and two more for Aunt Belleville to whip her into some sort of shape for our guests."

"Upon which time you will announce that not only have you agreed to take on the duties of Miss Darley's guardian, but you have become her betrothed as well," Beck urged hopefully.

"Exactly," Fletcher agreed, pushing Beck toward the door. "Unless, of course, I decide to strangle her instead. Now, my friend, excuse me, but you will please go away now. Billy Belchem will be joining me soon to help me with my bath."

Beck stumbled as he felt himself being propelled out of the room. "Help you with your bath? But she . . . But you . . . But, Fletch, no! I should say not. You can't do that!"

"Oh yes I can, Beck. Would you care to make a wager of it?" Fletcher asked him, looking down the hallway to see Rosalie approaching, a sullen look on her rather dirty face. "Ah, Billy, you have come to join me. How nice. And you have settled in comfortably, I trust? Come say hello to Beck, who is just leaving. You may not see him again, for I am thinking of sending him to inspect a small estate of mine in Jamaica."

"Fletch, you wouldn't," Beck muttered beneath his breath.

"Try me," Fletcher warned, his smile bright although his gray eyes were cold. "That sculpture you were eyeing in London against a trip to Jamaica."

Beck took a deep breath, let it out slowly, and turned to look at Rosalie Darley. He had seen the groom before, but had never really taken the time to do more than glance in Rosalie's general direction.

But now, with his secret knowledge to guide him, Beck could see that, although small and slight, there existed a definitely appealing form to her body, as well as a fine, strong little face that, once re-introduced to soap and water, might just prove to be extremely attractive.

All that to one side, the thought of Rosalie Darley—tidied up to look like a woman, or even remaining as she appeared now—becoming the victim of one of Fletcher's pranks was still infinitely more appealing to Beck than either the sculpture or the chance of a sea voyage to Jamaica.

"Your master has need of you," Beck intoned gruffly, turning away as the sight of Rosalie's large green eyes began to do strange things to his backbone. What was a little seasickness, compared to the look in those eyes? He took three steps down the hallway before turning back to add meaningfully, "I'll be just down the hall, in my room, if anyone should need me."

"So loyal, and so nearly brave," Fletcher crooned, waving Beck on his way as he pulled Rosalie into the chamber and firmly shut the door. "And now, halfling," he continued as he walked to the center of the room and untied the tasseled sash of his burgundy banyan, "might I believe that you have come prepared to begin your new duties?"

8

Rosalie looked warily about the room, her senses quivering like those of an alert hare that has just picked up the scent of a nearby fox.

It was a large chamber, with a prominent bed pushed against one wall; a thoroughly masculine room that intrigued her even as it intimidated her. The paintings, hangings, and furniture were all distinctly male, with no hint of any softening feminine influence, but attractive just the same.

The bed bothered her most, and the obviously full bathtub sitting before the cold fireplace. For someone who had been dreaming of spending the remainder of her life relaxing in just such a contraption, it amazed her how she now dreaded the mere sight of the thing.

Her gaze darted apprehensively to the bathtub and the extra pails of rinse water standing ready beside it, then back to Fletcher, now divested of his banyan, who stood in front of her dressed only in flowing white shirt and breeches.

"You've just bathed?" she ventured desperately, noticing that his thick blond locks were unruly, but not damp.

"No."

"You've had your tub brought in so that I may have

a bath?'' She knew her question seriously stretched the imagination, but hope wasn't a crime, was it?

''No, again.''

Her heart sank to her toes. ''You—you're going to bathe?''

''Third time lucky, halfling,'' Fletcher congratulated her brightly, slowly beginning to unbutton his shirt, so that his broad, hairy bare chest came into view.

''I—I'll go then,'' Rosalie stammered, turning for the door.

Fletcher's next words effectively stopped Rosalie in her tracks. ''Yet again, brat, you unman me with your overweening modesty, not to mention your total disregard for your new duties in this household. You will not be going anywhere. You're going to assist me with my bath.''

Rosalie wildly searched for a way out of her dilemma. ''About—about this new arrangement, sir,'' she said quickly. ''I've been down the hall in the lovely room you've given me, and I've been very careful not to sit anywhere, as I wouldn't want to soil anything. And I've been thinking. Hedge, well, he really does need me, sir.''

''And I do not?'' Fletcher broke in, two more buttons falling open.

''W-e-ll,'' Rosalie squeaked, her gaze riveted to Fletcher's bare chest and the soft down of blond hair, ''I suppose I just feel guilty, sir. Yes! That's it. I feel guilty. I mean, what with the gelding being spavined and everything, and—and all those horses. We have to work dawn to dusk with the two of us working. However will Hedge be able to manage without me.''

"I commend your devotion to Hedge, who I am sure would be gratified to hear it. However, as I have already assigned another lad to the stables, you can set your mind at rest."

Fletcher knew his actions must seem heartless, watching as Rosalie's small shoulders slumped, but he refused to give into the pity he felt for her. After all, had he detected any betraying signs of that emotion in her beautiful green eyes while he'd made a rare cake of himself, all but drooling over her when he believed her to be a boy?

No, he hadn't.

The snow-white shirt slid silently to the carpet and Fletcher's hands dropped to the buttons on his breeches.

A look of utter astonishment on her face, Rosalie turned her back and squeezed her eyes tightly shut, wondering if she were about to go stark, staring mad. Why didn't she stop him? Why didn't she say something, anything—even tell him the truth, confess her deception, put an end to this nonsense? What perverse imp kept her silent?

The slight noises behind her could only mean that Fletcher had removed his breeches, to become as naked as he had been the night he'd slipped into bed beside her at the inn. A moment later the sloshing sound of water being displaced told her that Fletcher had stepped into the tub.

She opened her eyes, believing it might be possible that she would be able to think better if she could see, and looked straight into the mirror that hung above a small bureau.

"Oh, my Lord," she whispered soundlessly, her jaw dropping open.

The mirror reflected the room at an angle, gifting her with no more than a glimpse of Fletcher's bare thigh as he sank into the tub, until all that remained visible were his head, his extremely broad, well-defined shoulders, and one bare arm.

She would burn in hell forever and ever. She had become depraved, morally bankrupt, the most wicked, perverted, brazen hoyden ever born, but she could not drag her gaze away from that mirror. She believed she could actually begin to feel herself sinking farther and farther into the murky but definitely exciting depths of depravity.

"Oh, Bil-ly."

Fletcher's lilting voice shot through Rosalie like a bolt of white-hot lightning as the strong premonition of impending disaster that had been with her all day exploded in her brain. "What?" she exclaimed, her voice unnaturally shrill.

"It occurs to me that I might need some help with my back."

Rosalie's small hands bunched into fists, as it occurred to her that, if a person were to do murder, they could only hang that person once. "You—you want me to put soap on—on your person?" she asked, grimacing at the inanity of her last words.

"On my person? That would be one way of putting it," Fletcher responded with a chuckle, knowing himself to be safely submerged beneath a concealing layer of bubbles, and not averse to stretching out his little game as far as Rosalie dared.

Rosalie continued to be a puzzle to him, and it was not only to pay her out for taking him in like a goose that he had determined to play out this little farce.

She had traveled alone in the district, for one thing—something gently reared females definitely did not do.

She had been sleeping in the Lakeview stables for more than a month, with none but Hedge for company.

Her language was not of the best, nor her general attitude.

Although she might show signs of maidenly modesty, she hadn't seemed at all shocked to see the barmaid at the inn in bed with a man.

In short, Fletcher could not be quite sure exactly what Rosalie Darley was. He knew who she was, and could admit to being intrigued by her, attracted to her, and not overly disappointed that his tenure as a bachelor showed all the damning signs of being about to come to an end.

She was William Darley's sister, and they didn't come any better than William. If William said his sister had been gently nurtured, then she had been well-raised and taught well enough to know that she was being thoroughly compromised by her guardian and had been repeatedly almost from the moment they had met.

He had to believe that Rosalie was just a high-spirited, still-innocent hoyden. Any other answer was unacceptable. But still, he had to be sure.

Fletcher could feel his muscles tensing as he looked across the room to where Rosalie stood, her back still turned to him. Her calves were shapely above the large, ugly boots, and he could, with his excellent imagination, picture the delicate shape of her bound-to-be-slim ankles.

Her hair, nearly as dark and sleek as Pagan's coat—although not nearly so well groomed—could be a true crowning glory once it was washed and tamed into some sort of style. His eyes narrowed as he contemplated the changes a soft, clinging gown would make, then he deliberately cleared his mind.

What was he doing? He was sitting, naked, in his bath, with the young woman he had been fashioning romantic fantasies about standing directly across the room. Maybe Beck had put his finger on the problem: perchance, just perchance, he was crazy.

Just as Fletcher determined to open his mouth, ordering Rosalie out of the room, she turned and walked, head high, toward the tub, the aristocrat marching bravely to the guillotine.

"I will need the soap," she said, looking somewhere to the left of the top of his head, her expression so woebegone that he knew his never fully developed fears for her chastity had been unfounded. He had to put a stop to this, now. He couldn't possibly go through with his plan to humiliate her.

"Never mind, halfling," he said, careful not to disturb the thinning layer of bubbles covering his lower body. "Just poor a bucket of hot water down my back and then retire until we meet again at dinner. I can see that you're weary."

Rosalie could feel her teeth begin to clench. That was all? That was it? He had driven her to the very brink of hysteria, just to send her away? Granted, Fletcher couldn't know exactly what he was doing, exactly who she was, for Rosalie, in the confidence of youth, could not believe that Fletcher had indeed succeeded in penetrating her disguise. As far as she was concerned, he had merely teased her because it was in his nature to enjoy teasing people.

Thinking her to be Billy Belchem, runaway, Fletcher

believed himself to be getting some of his own back for the pain Rosalie Darley, another runaway, had brought him. That was the only reason Rosalie could come up with for his behavior, and it appeared, at least to Rosalie, a reasonable explanation.

But now, goaded beyond endurance by Fletcher's little game, Rosalie forgot her crushing embarrassment, forgot her licentious, betraying thoughts, cast aside her recent vows to behave herself, and acted purely on impulse.

"More water, you said?" she asked sweetly, dipping her forefinger into one of the pails to check on the temperature of its contents. "My only happiness in life remains to please you, sir."

Fletcher, who had quietly been congratulating himself for having withstood temptation, started up as Rosalie's too-sweet voice and ridiculous subservience warned him—too late—of her intentions. There was nowhere to go, not unless he wished to stand up, which he most definitely did not want to do.

And so, his eyes squeezed shut, his shoulders hunched forward as if to ward off an attacker, Fletcher gritted his teeth and waited for the inevitable.

His wait was mercifully short. Within a matter of a heartbeat, a forceful waterfall of ice-cold liquid cascaded over his head, ran into his ears and mouth, and splashed off his bare back.

"Oh, dear," he heard Rosalie exclaim in patently false accents of horror while Fletcher bit his tongue so that he would not cry out. "What a lamentable accident! I do believe I might have picked up the wrong bucket. That was cold water, wasn't it? How can you ever forgive me?"

His teeth chattering, Fletcher desperately tried to

gather the scattered bubbles toward his chest, gritting tightly, "It's no matter, brat. Just go now, please, and I'll finish by myself."

"Of course, sir," Rosalie piped up, happy once more. "But I won't be able to join you for dinner, as I have no clothes fit for the table. I'll take my mutton with Hedge in the kitchens, as usual, sir." She turned to leave the room, throwing the only towel in the room to him without warning, so that it landed in front of him, in the water. "Good day to you, sir."

The moment the door closed behind Rosalie, Fletcher leapt from the tub, shivering and with nary a single romantic thought left in his wet head, to dive into his banyan, once more convinced that any punishment he had devised for her was totally justified—and probably not strong enough.

Lethbridge was confused. His master had installed a scruffy stable boy in the house, spouting some nonsense about the untrained boy serving as his personal servant. Yet the boy was assigned to one of the best bedchambers and not the attic servant quarters, as should be the case. As a matter of fact, the boy's room was better than the butler's own small chamber and sitting room, located just behind the pantry.

Added to this, the boy was still eating his evening meal with Hedge, who ate later than the rest of the servants because no one wanted to sit downwind of the bandy-legged Cockney.

Beck, whom Lethbridge had approached with his questions concerning this arrangement, had been less than useless, muttering only that all would be explained shortly, an explanation that was not sufficient to satisfy either the butler's curiosity or his injured sensibilities.

All the afternoon and evening Lethbridge had pondered this new problem, which, added to his master's bizarre—in the butler's opinion—behavior ever since returning from the fleshpots of London, worried the old man more than he could say.

Well, perhaps not more than he could say, for he, after soul-searching all through the dinner hour, at last approached Aunt Belleville with his concern once that dear woman had retired to the yellow saloon while Fletcher and Beck lingered over brandy and cigars in the dining room. At that time he expounded on his fears at some length.

Contrary to the reaction Lethbridge had expected—nay, hoped for—the lady did not fall on his neck, weeping in fear for her beloved nephew's sanity. No, indeed.

"Ill, you say, Lethbridge?" Aunt Belleville exclaimed, clasping her hands tightly at her waist then rubbing her palms together in what looked most suspiciously like unholy glee. "The poor dear! The poor, poor dear! It was the war, you know, Lethbridge." She leaned forward. "Oh, yes. It has to be. I've heard about this a dozen times or more. His wits are temporarily deranged from all the torment a soldier sees, all the carnage. Isn't it above everything wonderful?"

Lethbridge couldn't believe the woman had heard him correctly—or, for that matter, that he could have heard her correctly. "But, madam, only think," he stammered, taken aback, "this is terrible. What are we, who love him, to do? Poor Master Fletcher should have our pity."

"Yes, yes, of course," Aunt Belleville agreed quickly, clapping Lethbridge just above the elbow, for that was as high on his person as she could reach without extending herself. "Our pity. But more than that, Lethbridge," she added, her eyes sparkling as she cheered herself with the thought that the gilt ceiling in the music room was still possible to obtain, "Fletcher must have my care—my personal, undivided, extended care."

At last Lethbridge understood, and a slow smile creased his thin, poxmarked cheeks. He bowed in Aunt Belleville's direction, acknowledging her clear if self-centered thinking. "He wishes the boy summoned to the yellow saloon in a few minutes, madam, most probably so that the two of you should meet, and you shall have a chance to observe your nephew's actions firsthand, seeing them at last through informed eyes. But you must be brave, madam, for he can appear, as I have said, rather queer."

Aunt Belleville barely heard him, as she was already busy mentally running down her store of medicines in search of the one cure that was sure to work—eventually. Even as she applied her mind to that project, a part of her was recounting the contents of her sewing basket, wondering if her supply of colored thread was sufficient to embroider a pair of slippers for her patient. She could always send a servant to the village for more, the amount to be added to her nephew's bill, as usual. Wasn't it nice that Fletcher had only gone mad and not been rendered penniless!

"Tell me more about this stable boy, Lethbridge," she ordered after a moment, settling herself once more on the settee. "He is not taking undue advantage of my nephew's derangement, is he? I mean, he has not asked for anything, has he?"

The butler shook his head. "Only a bath, madam, which I, of course, refused. No need to encourage the lad to put on airs, watching while his betters race about carrying pails for him. And he seems to dislike his new position, still choosing to eat with Hedge rather than the other household servants."

"I see," Aunt Belleville responded, not seeing at all, for, if she should find her station in life suddenly elevated, she would most certainly not be timid in taking what was offered with both hands, even if it were only the chance to sit at a higher table. "Yet you say the boy is to be brought in here, to sit with the family." She looked up at the butler. "He—he isn't too dirty, I should hope?"

"His hands and face are clean, and Master Fletcher ordered me to supply a clean shirt, madam, and—and unmentionables."

"Good." Aunt Belleville relaxed slightly, for she was not looking forward to spending the remainder of the evening with her scented handkerchief pressed to her nostrils. "Now be quiet, Lethbridge. I believe I hear my nephew approaching and he mustn't learn that we have been discussing him."

Lethbridge bowed once more, reluctant to leave the one woman who had ever showed herself to be kindly disposed to him, but aware that his presence in the yellow saloon could no longer be justified.

As the butler passed out of the room, Fletcher, who had entered through another doorway across the room, called out to him, reminding him that young Billy Belchem was to join them shortly.

"And don't take no for an answer," Fletcher added warningly, watching as Lethbridge's bony shoulders stiffened.

"Billy Belchem?" Aunt Belleville questioned, seeing her opportunity and grabbing at it with both hands. "I wasn't told we were to have an after-dinner guest. How very delightful. Beck, take a moment to look at Fletcher, if you please. Don't you think he appears to be rather pale?"

Beck, who had just spent a half-hour vainly trying to convince Fletcher to give up his plan to put Rosalie through hoops and have done with his foolishness—all to no avail—was more than happy to agree with the lady. Threaten him with a voyage to Jamaica, would he? Well, Beck had a way to pay him out for that one. "Yes, madam, I had noticed it," he agreed solemnly. "I believe your nephew got himself a bit of a soaking this afternoon and may have taken a chill."

"Wretch," Fletcher said quietly, wondering why he had bothered to tell Beck what had happened, only so that man could hold the incident over his head.

"A soaking?" Aunt Belleville was confused, for the entire day had been fine—a rare occurrence in the district—with nary a drop of rain. "Too much water is not salutiferous to the body," she warned, shaking her head. "Why, my dear neighbor in Bath . . . Have I ever told you I once resided in Bath? I did, you know, for several months, while Cousin Albert was dying. But that is nothing to the point, is it? My neighbor made a religion of bathing every day, even though I warned him against it, and he died before his time."

"You spent some months in Bath? I hadn't realized, dearest lady, what a giddy life you've had." Fletcher shot a decidedly mischievous look at Beck. "What a waste, Aunt, that this gentleman—and Cousin Albert, of course—should have died. How old was he—the gentleman, that is?"

The lady gave a deep sigh. "No more than sixty," she answered, shaking her head. "And we were becoming such dear friends."

Chuckling silently, Fletcher marveled at the lengths a man would go to escape Aunt Belleville's ministrations. Dying seemed to be a step or two too far, but then he had only been the object of his aunt's smothering ministrations, and not her subtle amorous advances.

Hearing a slight commotion at the rear of the house—most probably caused by Lethbridge's attempts to bring Rosalie to the yellow saloon as per his instructions—Fletcher leaned forward in his chair to address his aunt. "As I was saying, my dear, we will be joined shortly by young Master Billy Belchem, my companion while traveling about the district these past days. You may remember stepping on him the day I arrived from London. Anyway, I discovered, while we were traveling, that he is not what he pretends to be."

Aunt Belleville was nonplussed. "He—he only pretends to be a stable boy?" she asked, clearly incredulous. "Why would anyone wish to do anything as silly as that? I mean, if a person were to pretend he was someone he isn't, wouldn't it be much nicer to pretend he was someone important? I know I should, if I were of a mind to pretend I was someone I wasn't, although I never would, would I? Would you, Beck? No, of course not. Who would? It makes no sense." She squinted at Fletcher. "Are you quite sure you shouldn't be lying down, nephew?"

Beck, who had been doing his possible to preserve

his countenance with an iron will he was sure even Wellington would admire, discreetly hid his smile behind his handkerchief. If Fletcher was having this much trouble explaining half Rosalie's story to his aunt, being present while Fletcher told her the whole would be a treat he wouldn't wish to miss.

A noise outside in the foyer interrupted all their thoughts, if indeed they were still having any, for it had been a most confusing conversation, and the doors opened to admit a rather disheveled Lethbridge.

"Sirs, madam—Master Belchem," he all but growled, reaching behind him to catapult Rosalie roughly into the room by way of her shirt sleeve. "Shall I bring in the tea tray now, and would you perhaps like a glass of warmed milk for this scamp—this boy?"

"Poor Lethbridge appears upset," Fletcher commented to Beck. "Must be his diet that makes him so cranky, don't you think?"

Rosalie angrily shook herself free of the butler, who had refused to listen to her several very good reasons why she should not be sent to the yellow saloon, and strode purposefully across the room to confront Fletcher.

"To what purpose are you doing this?" she railed, uncaring that she was most probably making a thorough idiot of herself. "You're mad as Bedlam, do you know that?" She turned to face Beck and Aunt Belleville and repeated, "He's mad as Bedlam."

Hearing her private diagnosis spoken aloud did wonders for Aunt Belleville's formerly negative opinion of the stable boy. Patting the empty cushion beside her, she said kindly, "Come sit down by me, little boy, and I shall have Lethbridge bring you the milk he has so kindly suggested."

Eyeing the older woman warily and not seeing any malice in her eyes—nor much real intelligence, for that matter—Rosalie shot one last, stunning look at Fletcher and then did as she was bid, muttering her thanks as she sat herself gingerly on the edge of the settee. She had promised Hedge she would behave, and she owed the man at least that much.

A decidedly uncomfortable silence followed, during which time Lethbridge personally rolled in the tea cart and placed the silver service in front of Aunt Belleville.

Although no words were spoken aloud, entire volumes passed back and forth between Fletcher and Beck, Aunt Belleville and Lethbridge, and Rosalie and herself, who felt no real lapse in not having a partner with which to exchange meaningful glances, as she was always comfortable making conversation with her imagination.

Once the tea had been served and the butler had withdrawn, albeit reluctantly, with one last, long imploring look passing between he and Aunt Belleville, Fletcher spoke. "There now, everyone," he commented jovially, just as if no undercurrents existed and they were just four people enjoying their tea, "isn't this cozy? Billy, does this bring back any memories of your life before taking to the road? Does it make the thought of being transported to your aunt's home in Tunbridge Wells any more palatable?"

"Not if you intend to have evening prayers," Rosalie grumbled meanly, staring at her toes and remembering the cuff on the head and lengthy homily Lethbridge had given her for daring to enter the house in her muddy boots. She shrank back on the settee as Beck gave out a shout of laughter.

She felt more exposed, more vulnerable, than she had

before, the perpetual smuts on her face now washed away, and found it unbelievable that Aunt Belleville, if no one else, could not see through her disguise. Was she so plain, so boringly ordinary, that none of the three of them, plus Lethbridge, had been inclined to look at her closely?

Silence reigned once more as Fletcher, who was enjoying himself immensely, made no move to make Rosalie feel comfortable, and Beck, who was afraid to say anything for fear Rosalie would say something else outrageous, concentrated on his teacup.

Aunt Belleville, having taken a good look at Rosalie and decided that the stable boy's appearance in the house was merely a symptom of her nephew's malady, and not the cause of it, cudgeled her brain for another topic of conversation that might shed some light on Fletcher's problems.

"Have you heard any more about this missing Rosalie person you asked about the other day, dear?" she asked, remembering Fletcher's volatile mood when he had heard about the existence of a letter mentioning that name. "You never did say anything about it again, now that I think on it, but then I was called away to minister to Mrs. Kelsey's cough, wasn't I, and we really haven't had much time for a comfortable coze since then, have we?"

Rosalie felt her throat constrict. Fletcher hadn't told his aunt that he had become her guardian? Was it so unimportant to him? Or had he, after downing several bottles of strong spirits and indulging himself in an orgy of self-pity, chosen to ignore William's letter?

"You didn't tell your own aunt that William Darley named you as guardian to his only sister, Rosalie?"

Beck questioned archly, looking at his friend. "But wasn't it she who first read the letter from Mrs. Beale?"

Mrs. Beale. How Rosalie hated hearing that woman's name spoken aloud. Her small hands bundled into fists. The woman had somehow found her out. How could that be? Even though Fletcher had mentioned the woman's name that night in the stables, Rosalie still found it difficult to believe the woman possessed the wit to link her disappearance to Lakeview. She had thought she had covered her tracks so well.

Yet Mrs. Beale had only written a letter. It wasn't as if she and Sawyer were actually here, at Lakeview. Rosalie bit her lip, her head still down, and waited for Fletcher to speak.

She was to be disappointed, for Aunt Belleville, who had been sitting very still, exploded, "Your ward! Fletcher! You never said a word. You mean to tell me . . . No, obviously you never meant to tell me. How can you sit there so calmly when your ward has gone missing? That's what the letter said. The little girl has gone missing, run away from her home. I don't understand this. You bring a stable boy into the house in anticipation of returning him to his family in Tunbridge Wells, but you do not lift a finger to rescue a poor, helpless female who remains out in the wide world somewhere, in terrible danger."

"Now, Aunt," Fletcher tried to interrupt, but the woman was having none of it.

Her handkerchief was frantically waving beneath her chin as she fanned her flushed features. "I don't want to hear it, Fletcher. Lethbridge said you were all about in your head, but it is more than that, worse than that. You are unconscionable. Where are your senses? Where are your priorities? Where is my hartshorn? I believe I feel faint."

"I've written to Mrs. Beale, Aunt," Fletcher succeeded in slipping in at last, "and she should be joining us here at Lakeview within a matter of days. Until then, there remains less than nothing I can do. How can I locate this Rosalie when I don't know her age or what she looks like? If, in the meantime, I am making myself useful by helping Billy here, it is only to keep myself busy, and my mind occupied."

Aunt Belleville appeared to be slightly mollified. "You don't know her age? I don't believe I understand any of this. Exactly who was William Darley, and why should the gentleman have left the care of his sister to you? He was a gentleman, wasn't he?"

While Rosalie tried to make herself disappear into the cushions of the settee, at the same time cudgeling her brain for a way to disappear from Lakeview before Mrs. Beale's arrival, Fletcher gave his aunt a pithy explanation, beginning with Beck's discovery of the letter from William and ending with the words, ". . . only to have found that the abominable brat I have been saddled with has run off somewhere."

Rosalie lifted her gaze to see the furnishings of the yellow saloon through an angry red haze, all thoughts of running away in the middle of the night forgotten. Abominable brat, was she? Saddled, was he? Her spine stiffened. She had been right to come here unannounced and disguised, to see for herself what sort of man Fletcher Belden was.

And now, at last, she knew. He didn't want her. At least horrid Mrs. Beale wanted her, although being the guest of honor at a Black Mass was not exactly Rosalie's idea of the way in which she most desired to be "wanted."

While Aunt Belleville fretted aloud over menus and sleeping arrangements for Mrs. Beale once that woman had arrived at Lakeview, interrupting herself several times to point out to Fletcher that she, his loving, ever-willing aunt, would do all her possible to be a good chaperone to young Rosalie once that lamentably misplaced child was found, Fletcher watched Rosalie's face intently, disliking the set look of her jaw and the deep, cold green of her eyes.

She was hating him very much at the moment, a thought that displeased him intensely. It wasn't as if he had developed a deathless passion for the girl—he'd hardly had time for that—but he didn't relish being the object of her disgust.

Perhaps the "abominable brat" part of his story had been a little overdone. He should have sounded more upset, more concerned for her welfare, and less put upon by William's request.

Just as he was about to interrupt Aunt Belleville in the midst of her mental redecoration of Arabella's bedchamber for Rosalie, Fletcher's pride silenced him. Why was he feeling guilty? Had he run away from home to come checking up on her so that, if he found her to be unappealing, he could cry off from what had come to be William's dying request?

No, he certainly had not. The fact that he hadn't known of Rosalie's existence proved nothing to the point, for he knew that, as a man of honor, the thought of turning his back on her would never have entered his head.

Besides, he was going to marry her, wasn't he? If

Beck's gloomy predictions hadn't been enough to make him see he had compromised the girl, his memory of the effect her soft body and intelligent belligerence had on him was enough to tell him that marriage to Rosalie was the only answer that made any sense.

Yet there she sat, hating him, judging him. Didn't she know what she had put him through with her innocent deception? Had she no idea of the consequences her refusal to identify herself to him would bring down on both their heads?

No. No, she didn't. She really didn't know. So sure she had fooled him, it doubtless had not yet occurred to her that she had crossed a fine line past which there could be no return. Fletcher chewed on this revelation for a moment, savoring it, and then spoke, completely changing the subject from Aunt Belleville's discussion of the proper care of young females in a male household—which had a lot to do with having an older, sensible woman in constant residence—to one that, at the moment, lay much closer to his heart.

"Beck," he said, turning to his friend, who was looking as if he might burst at any moment, "do you remember Bourne?"

"Bourne?" Beck repeated, still half-lost in a brown study that had a lot to do with leaving Lakeview in order to lead a more peaceful life, perhaps in deepest Africa, where the greatest danger lay in being mistaken for lunch by some hungry lion, and not having to worry about pathetically appealing green eyes and a tiny, sad face. "You mean the earl? What about him?"

Fletcher rose, walking to the drinks table to pour himself a brandy. "Oh, nothing really. I was thinking about Rosalie, my ward, and it occurred to me that, as I don't know her age, she might be old enough to have compromised herself somewhere along the way as she roams about the countryside. That's how Bourne got his wife, if you remember. Kissed her in the Home Wood, not knowing her true identity, and—presto!—poor Kit found himself leg-shackled."

Rosalie's head snapped back, her green eyes wide as saucers, causing Fletcher no end of satisfaction. "He—he had to marry her simply because he kissed her? One kiss?" she squeaked, then quickly lowered her head once more.

"That's all it takes, halfling," Fletcher said, winking to Beck, who began to feel better about his friend. "Remember that, both of you, if you should ever think about kissing a girl, although it pleases me to report that Kit and his wife are very happy. Oh, but no, I remember now. You, er, 'ain't in the petticoat line,' are you, Billy?"

"Richard Casterbridge kissed me in the arbor behind the rectory," Aunt Belleville put in dreamily, then sobered. "Only once, mind you, and I allowed it only because I had reached three-and-twenty and no one else had ever asked. But I never told anyone, as I had decided we wouldn't suit."

"Aunt," Fletcher exclaimed, a hand to his chest. "There is a young boy in the room."

The woman colored, tipping her head to one side. "It was only a kiss, Fletcher," she pointed out. "It wasn't as if I had . . . as if we had . . . you know what I mean, nephew."

"Shared a bed? Slept together? Seen each other in a state of undress? Been alone together, in a wood, or an inn, with no chaperone, no notions of propriety? Can that be the sort of thing you meant, Aunt?'' Fletcher persevered, knowing that any ideas he'd had of stringing out Rosalie's little deception for so much as another minute had all gone by the board, and the time for truth had come.

Rosalie hopped to her feet, her face as white as freshly washed wool. ''You,'' she accused in dreadful tones, pointing one trembling finger at Fletcher. ''You know! You know, and you did this on purpose. Didn't you?''

''Know?'' Aunt Belleville looked at Fletcher and then at Beck. ''What does he know? What is the boy talking about?''

''How long have you known?'' Rosalie demanded, taking a menacing step toward Fletcher. ''Did you know when we were at the inn? No, you couldn't have. You wouldn't have made such a complete ass of yourself talking about all the wonderfully masculine things you have done if you had known. And to think I felt sorry for you. How could I have been so blind? Something happened after that. When, Fletcher? When did you know?''

''Yes, when Fletcher?'' Beck slid in, also rising. ''And I think I want to hear more about this business of your being a complete ass. I've long suspected it, but I really would like to have it confirmed.''

Fletcher silenced Beck with a look, turning away only as Rosalie went on the attack once more.

''Your relevation came after we returned to Lakeview, didn't it?'' she concluded correctly, knowing she had hit on the truth by the way his gray eyes slid away from hers for a moment. ''You unspeakable cad! It did. This—this,'' she sputtered, waving her arms to include the yellow saloon, her bedchamber, and most probably, the entirety of Lakeview, "was all a great big hum. A farce you perpetrated for your own amusement. But how? How did you know?"

It was as if the two of them were alone in the room. Neither paid any attention to Beck, who continued to enjoy himself immensely; Aunt Belleville, who sat on the settee, resembling nothing more than a spectator at a fiercely contested tennis match; or Lethbridge, who had crept into the room and who now hung on Rosalie's every word.

Fletcher took another step forward, staring deeply into her eyes. "The other night, in the stables, you told me not to worry that my ward had not yet arrived, as it is a long way here from Patterdale."

Rosalie didn't understand. "So? What is that to the point?"

Fletcher smiled, realizing he liked feeling superior to Rosalie for this one moment, relishing the knowledge that, for once in their tempestuous association, he held the upper hand. "I hadn't told you Rosalie lived in Patterdale, halfling," he informed her, addressing her by what, to him, had become a form of endearment.

He watched as Rosalie recounted the last few days in her mind, separating events as to their day and time. It wouldn't be long now, he thought patiently as he saw her become, if possible, even more pale than she had been before.

When she spoke, her voice was quiet, hardly more than a whisper. "You let me see you naked after you knew who I am."

Rosalie's voice had been low, but it had carried to Aunt Belleville's ears, and she had picked up on one, most telling word. "Naked? Who was naked?"

Fletcher turned to his aunt. "I'm sorry, dearest lady, have we confused you? I'll explain. You see, Billy here is not really Billy. He's Rosalie. Actually, she's Rosalie. You'll have to forgive me, but it's deuced difficult keeping my tongue straight with all these hes and shes.

"All that to one side, it would appear that, as I did not show up at Hilltop Farm to claim my ward—not knowing that I had one, as you'll recall—my ward decided, for reasons of her own, which I shall be gratified to learn, to come to Lakeview. She did this disguised as Billy Smith, later to be known as Billy Belchem, but don't bother your head about all that, madam, for all you need to know is that this delightful though slightly dusty creature in front of you is none other than Rosalie Darley, William's sister, my ward and, as soon as may be, my wife."

"Your wife!"

This exclamation was extremely loud, coming simultaneously as it did out of the mouths of Rosalie and Lethbridge, who had so forgotten himself as to walk into the room until he ended standing no more than three feet behind Fletcher.

Unfortunately, the butler had not positioned himself close enough to do more than watch as Aunt Belleville, who, instead of joining the chorus of "Your wife," had screeched tragically, "My gilt ceiling!" before drooping against the settee cushions in a dead faint.

9

In the end, not evening prayers—nor much else of any import, for that matter—took place at Lakeview that night, the evening ending most abruptly once Aunt Belleville had regained her senses, espied Rosalie, and all but dragged that still-simmering young woman out of the yellow saloon by the tip of her right ear, leaving Beck to read a pithy lecture to his childhood friend on the folly of ever believing there existed in this entire world a single woman with so much as a piddling appreciation of humor.

By midmorning of the following day none save the Belden household servants had made an appearance downstairs, the inhabitants of Lakeview whose station allowed them to breakfast in their rooms taking full advantage of that luxury, most probably in the hope that this simple strategy would keep them from an unlooked-for encounter with anyone who might be inclined to either ring a peal over their heads or pop them one in the nose.

Lakeview had taken on all the less-charming qualities of an armed camp, with the women firmly pitted against the men, and only the politic Lethbridge feeling any charity toward Fletcher, who, when it came to being the proclaimed villain of the piece, definitely bore off the palm.

"Well, I think it to be just famous, sir. Allow me to be the only—I mean, the first to felicitate you on your upcoming nuptials," Lethbridge had said the night before, after all the other occupants of the yellow saloon save Fletcher had departed in high dudgeon to go their own way.

"And once she has time to ponder this unsettling development for a time," the man had continued bravely, "I do believe the old girl—that is to say, your aunt—will most assuredly come to appreciate the many benefits to be derived from such an unexpected situation."

He retired to his bed with only this faint praise to speed him to his rest—as it had never occurred to Fletcher that his betrothal, once it had come, would be viewed as an "unsettling development," and it can be no wonder that when he finally did deign to appear in the yellow saloon just before noon, Fletcher entered warily, looking about to assure himself that no one lay in wait, prepared to ambush him.

Ringing for Lethbridge, he sat himself down in his favorite chair and waited for that man to bring him the newspaper Fletcher had, upon rising, found to have already been delivered, at the young lady's request, to Rosalie's chamber.

For someone who had been bedding down in an empty horse stall for several weeks, he had thought at the time, it appeared that his reluctant fiancée had encountered precious little difficulty in putting herself back into the role of lady of the household, demands for service and all.

A steaming cup of coffee at his right hand, Fletcher sat back and opened the newspaper, hoping to find something within its pages to capture his interest, diverting his mind from the intense hustle and bustle he knew to be going on upstairs, behind Aunt Belleville's door.

He read of Prinny's latest round of entertainments for the visiting dignitaries, who were still taking up precious space in the city, then shook his head at a small, well-hidden account of the plight of returning veterans of the war, who admitted to being a trifle overset as to the unconscionable amount of time it seemed to be taking for them to collect their back pay from a treasury sadly depleted first by the war and now by the Prince Regent's excesses.

Fletcher had just finished skimming an anonymous, obliquely risque account of "Lady J———y and the handsome Hussar, Lord W———r at Almack's" in one of the columns when, upon turning the page, he found himself confronted with a dessert-plate-sized hole smack in the center of his newspaper.

"What in blue blazes?" he complained aloud, noticing that the paper had been torn, rather than cut, and that the tear seemed to have been made by design rather than as the result of an accident. "Rosalie," he concluded in a heartbeat.

Rosalie Darley had done this. She had desecrated his precious newspaper, his only reliable contact with the world outside the Lake District. Wasn't it bad enough that the news contained in the week-old paper had already grown whiskers by the time he received it?

Wasn't it sufficient that he also had to cool his heels above an hour to read the bloody thing once it finally found its way to Lakeview? Did she then have to add insult to injury by chewing a whacking great hunk out of it before handing it over to him, the master of the house?

"Lethbridge," he roared, bringing that man into the room at a run. "Look at this!" Fletcher put his fist and forearm through the hole in his precious newspaper and waggled his fingers at the butler. "What's the meaning of this sacrilege? Good God, man, is nothing sacred anymore?

The butler, who had been standing just outside the door in anticipation of just such a summons, well aware of a gentleman's proprietary airs toward his newspaper, straightened his spine, lifted his chin, and swiftly dumped the blame where it belonged.

"It was Miss Darley, sir," he said, somehow maintaining his air of dignity while selling Rosalie out in order to preserve his own skin. "One of the items on the page must have caught her eye, sir. I—I had hoped you wouldn't notice."

"Wouldn't notice? Wouldn't notice! Oh, foul, foul! How could I not notice?" Fletcher exploded, his forearm still stuck through the aforementioned whacking great hole as he rose to angrily pace the carpet. He stopped in his tracks, setting his jaw, his gray eyes shooting darts that still lacked a target.

"I want it back," he grumbled, just like a pouting nursery tot who has just lost his new kite to a strong spring breeze. "Lethbridge, go upstairs right now, and tell Miss Darley, no, demand that Miss Darley return my paper to me."

Lethbridge sighed, already aware that it would be a futile mission. "I've tried, sir. She won't do it," he imparted sadly. "The missing part contains only an advertisement, she said, and would be of no possible interest to you."

"She said that, did she?" Fletcher felt himself to be by nature a peaceful man, a patient man, an undemanding man. He had borne up heroically when he had come to realize that, willing or not, he was honor-bound to marry Rosalie Darley.

But wait. Didn't he love her? Yes, of course he loved her. But that had nothing to do with the thing, dammit! He still had behaved beautifully. Why, he had even been willing to forgive Rosalie her ill-advised deception, her outrageous behavior, and her total lack of faith in him.

In point of fact, for that matter, he had, except for a certain regrettable lapse having to do with his hastily aborted trial by water yesterday afternoon with a bathtub full of bubbles, been a gentleman to his backbone.

So, why was he being treated this way? Why, indeed? Fletcher's eyelids puckered until his eyes were barely visible. His lips drew into a bow. His hands moved slowly, deliberately, as he shed himself of the newspaper, folded it, and deposited it carefully on a nearby table.

"Lethbridge?" he questioned tightly, his voice low and menacing.

"Sir?" the butler squeaked, for he had not seen such a pinched, determined look since before Fletcher's father had been laid to rest in the family mausoleum, may the good Lord rest his at times autocratic soul.

"Miss Darley, Lethbridge. She remains closeted with my aunt?"

"Yes, sir."

"Then one might safely assume that one might be able to enter Miss Darley's chamber unseen and liberate the scrap of paper now in question?"

Lethbridge nodded warily, then brightened. "It would certainly seem so, sir. Shall I go upstairs, sir, and—"

"You, Lethbridge?" Fletcher smiled devilishly, his eyebrows raised as he blinked three times in the butler's direction, reminding Lethbridge of nothing more than a cat that has just espied a nest of plump, juicy mice. "Oh, no, my friend. I wouldn't ask it of you, really. Please, allow me."

Fletcher sped up the broad staircase in the twinkling of a bedpost, steathily opening the door to Rosalie's assigned bedchamber before abandoning stealth to engage in a determined search of the room, convinced he had every right to do anything he needed to do to retrieve his conduit to the world, his most basic link to society, his paper and ink badge of authority: his newspaper!

As Rosalie's possessions were few and her occupation of the bedchamber not of any great length of time, it wasn't long before Fletcher had located the scrap of newspaper in the top drawer of the mahogany ladies' desk that stood in front of the large window that looked out over the gardens.

He glanced at the printed page, seeing that it contained random lines concerning two different news topics, and turned it over, expecting to discover a recipe for cucumber cream or some such nonsense, only to discover that Rosalie had indeed ripped out an advertisement.

And what an advertisement!

"Lost Happiness Regained," he read aloud, his brow puckering. "Any female involved in distress from an expectation of inevitable dishonor may obtain Consolation and Security, and meet with the motherly attention so necessary on those occasions for the restoration of that Security of Mind attendant on cultivated life, by communicating with Mrs. Rimston."

He read the advertisement twice, unbelieving the thunderbolts of rage that tore through his body as he realized the terrible message lurking behind the delicately structured phrases.

Fletcher collapsed into the straight-backed chair beside the desk, a broken, beaten man.

First Arabella, now Rosalie. Arabella had gotten with child thanks to her love for a French prisoner of war. His sister had chosen to destroy herself rather than shame her brother by gifting him with a bastard niece or nephew. Rosalie, it would seem, had chosen another path, one that would rid her of the child. How, he wondered dumbly, considering how innocent she appeared to be, had Rosalie gotten with child in the first place?

Fletcher shook his head. "No," he berated himself cynically, "you already know how she came to be in this condition. You just don't know who." A name came, unbidden, into his head: Sawyer. He and Mrs. Beale, according to William's letter, seem to go hand in hand. Perhaps he assaulted Rosalie, and that's why she ran away. It's no great wonder she never realized that playing out her deception here at Lakeview had served to thoroughly compromise her so that we would have to marry: she had already been compromised up to her neck. Poor halfling!

And poor Fletcher. Had he been doomed to forever have such wretched luck with women? For, selfish as it might seem, a moment's thought told him that he felt very sorry for himself. He loved Rosalie, he was convinced of that fact, yet the very notion of acting as doting father to another man's offspring devastated him, bringing him almost as low as did the maddening thought that his darling Rosalie had suffered the indignity of another man's attentions.

Fletcher felt physically ill and was moment by moment becoming angrier with himself. Rosalie needed him, really needed him, now more than ever. Besides, he owed it to William. He raised his head, casting off any remaining doubts, knowing what he had to do. He would go to her, tell her what he knew, and marry her at once. Not out of pity. Not out of duty. No. He would marry her because he loved her.

Rising to drag himself down the hallway to his aunt's room, Fletcher noticed that a letter lay in the open drawer. Rosalie had written a letter to someone? Who would she write to—if not the infamous Mrs. Rimston?

Feeling that there could be no real crime in reading the letter, and hopeful of discovering something more about Rosalie's dilemma than he already knew, he picked up the single page and, steeling his heart against the onslaught of pain that was sure to come, began to read.

A minute later he was once more seated in the desk chair—sprawled, actually—laughing so hard tears ran down his cheeks.

Fletcher had already installed himself in the dining room when the bell was rung for the usual informal buffet-style luncheon—for Lakeview was, at heart, a working farm—awaiting the promised appearance of his aunt and fiancée.

Beck entered the room first, which did not surprise Fletcher, for Beck had never been one to be the last to slip his legs beneath a table. "Fletch," he said, acknowledging his employer with a curt nod. "I've been wondering when you'd surface. Do you think you could join me for an inspection ride about the estate this afternoon? Unless you have in mind another upsetment of the ladies, of course, in which case I fully understand if you decide to cry off the task you have already successfully avoided since our return to Lakeview."

Fletcher eyed Beck appreciatively. "That was quite a speech, my friend," he commented with a nod of his head. "You always were civil as a nun's hen when angry. Feeling put upon, are you?"

His bravado successfully deflated by Fletcher's bantering tone, Beck sighed, saying, "I could do with a bit of help, yes, although the estate admittedly does all but run itself."

"But—" Fletcher prompted.

"But dash it, man—did you have to be so full of yourself last night, teasing the ladies that way? You're lucky your aunt didn't suffer a spasm, and as for Miss Darley, well, if I'm right about her, you're even more lucky that she didn't clunk you over the head with a vase or something. To announce, almost in one breath, both that her true identity was known to you, and your engagement . . . Well, I just think you overreached yourself."

Fletcher moved along the sideboard, loading his plate with thin slices of ham and various other foods meant to satisfy his extremely hearty appetite. "Would it please you to know, Beck, that I have suffered myself in this thing?"

Beck followed along behind, stabbing at a slice of ham with a silver serving fork. "It would," he agreed tersely.

Fletcher looked about the room, just to assure himself they were in no danger of being disturbed by either the ladies or some servant intent on replenishing one of the serving platters. He leaned toward his friend and said, "I found a letter in Miss Darley's desk, Beck. A letter to a certain Mrs. Rimston in Clerkwell, in answer to that woman's advertisement of services rendered in the newspaper."

"And?"

Fletcher leaned closer. "Mrs. Rimston," he whispered importantly, as if gifting Beck with the supreme secret of the universe, "is an acknowledged abortionist."

The china plate, piled high with ham, vegetables, a shelled boiled egg, and three slices of turkey, dropped to the floor, to shatter into six separate pieces. "A what!"

Looking down on the tangible evidence of Beck's shock upon hearing his news, Fletcher smiled, saying, "That closely mirrors my initial reaction. Thankfully," he added, putting down his own plate so that he could begin filling another for Beck, "Miss Darley's interpretation of Mrs. Rimston's advertisement meant to attract 'any female involved in distress from an expectation of inevitable dishonor' and in need of—and again, I quote—'the motherly attention so necessary on those occasions for the restoration of that Security of Mind attendant on cultivated life,' was not the one intended by this same Mrs. Rimston."

Beck watched helplessly as Fletcher placed a quantity of sliced cooked carrots, which Beck had never been able to abide, on the plate he was preparing for him. "How can you be sure?"

Fletcher handed over the plate, returning his attention

to his own, picking it up and heading for his chair at the head of the table. ''I can be sure, Beck, because I, feeling myself pushed past all concerns of discretion and personal privacy, took it upon myself to read the letter Miss Darley had composed to the woman, imploring her help.''

Beck prudently sat down before he fell down, stabbing a fork randomly in the direction of the plate, only to discover a moment later that he had just filled his mouth with cooked carrots. Pulling a face, he asked, ''What did she write?''

Fletcher chewed on a piece of ham for a few moments, trying to decide how long he could keep Beck dangling before the man went for his throat. ''Rosalie told Mrs. Rimston she had been compromised by a man who didn't really want her—she referred to me by name, you understand, adding also that she, dear thing, loves me to distraction and beyond—and then begged to be taken in by the woman until such time as she could publish a novel, or become an actress, or take a ship to America. Have I told you, Beck, that Rosalie seems to possess a rather vivid if not exceptional imagination?''

''Still,'' Beck said, eyeing his friend carefully, ''the whole thing must have given you quite a turn, Fletch, what with Arabella and all.'' He lowered his head, knowing he had spoken without thinking. ''Sorry. But—but it must be gratifying to know that Miss Darley thinks herself in love with you, I suppose?''

''Thinks herself in love with me, Beck?'' Fletcher frowned. ''You find that difficult to believe?''

Beck grinned, his appetite returned, his fears flown. ''Frankly, Fletch, I find it difficult to believe she hasn't murdered you in your bed.''

Fletcher's mouth opened, undoubtedly in preparation

of defending himself, when Aunt Belleville sailed into the room, her many flowing draperies in full flight. "There you are, you lucky, lucky man," she trilled, going to the end of the table to plant a kiss on her nephew's cheek. "Close your eyes, Fletcher—you too, Beck—and don't open them until I tell you to. All right?"

Fletcher eyed his aunt owlishly. The woman's pudgy cheeks were flushed, her small eyes twinkling. "What have you done, Aunt?" he asked facetiously. "I didn't miss anything, did I? I mean," he added, his gaze quickly scanning the dining room as if she had just topped her mangling of the yellow saloon with another outrageous redecoration and he had somehow overlooked it, "I don't see anything different in here. Beck, have you noticed anything?"

"You both will in a minute, you naughty boy," Aunt Belleville teased, giving him an affectionate slap on the shoulder, for she seemed in a mood that would forgive her nephew anything. "Fletcher, do what I said, please, and close your eyes. No peeking, now. Good! I have to tell you, Fletcher, you gave me quite a turn last night with your news, but you offered me quite a challenge as well—"

"I exist only to please you, Aunt," Fletcher broke in, his eyes still obediently shut.

"Oh, pooh, you do not. After spending a most unquiet night, I rose early this morning full of resolution. Have I told you, nephew, that Elsie, my abigail, has a most wonderful way with a scissors? Really, she has a veritable genius in her fingertips. Oh, dear," she exclaimed, espying Beck's broken plate on the floor. "Has someone had an accident? I should summon Lethbridge, I suppose—"

"Aunt, I warn you, if I keep my eyes closed much longer, they may just stick that way forevermore," Fletcher interrupted once more. "May I please open them now, or do you think you could possibly get to the point?"

Aunt Belleville only laughed at this silliness, for everyone knew a person's eyes couldn't stick that way—unless someone were to deliver a sharp smack to the back of that person's skull, that is. "Of course we had only one of your dear sister's outgrown gowns to work with, and would have needed the fal-lals of fashion and such to really do the thing right—ribbons, and bows, and perhaps some jewelry—but although I admit to having had some serious qualms at the outset, it is early days yet, and I see nothing but a continuing round of successes once I have the dressing of her firmly in hand. Beck, I saw that! You're peeking."

Squeezing his eyes closed once more, Beck explained that he really hadn't been looking. He had been attempting to eat and had opened one eye to make sure he wasn't about to wind up with another mouthful of carrots.

"Beck is starving, Aunt," Fletcher pointed out, doing his utmost not to laugh aloud. "It will, alas, be on your head if he faints into his plate, but if you aren't ready to unveil your success, as you've termed it, I'm sure Beck will be able to find it in his heart to forgive you."

Aunt Belleville sighed, giving up the fight. After all, there would be plenty of time for boasting once she had dazzled the gentlemen with her glorious creation. "Rosalie, you may come in."

There came a slight rustle at the doorway and Fletcher's heart began to pound uncomfortably in his chest. He knew what was about to happen. Only a brainless dolt could have heard the near riot and rumpus of activity that had maids running to and fro all morning from Aunt Belleville's bedchamber and not know. When he opened his eyes, Rosalie would be standing in front of him, no longer the scruffy stable boy, but as his affianced wife.

How would she look?

She would be clean, of that much he knew he could be certain, giving him only his second sight of her without a smudge of dirt appearing somewhere on her face. He had already seen her hair, that mangled tangle of roughly cut ebony, and Elsie's talents to one side, he held out little hope for much improvement there until it could grow into a more feminine style.

"My God," Fletcher heard Beck whisper, his voice husky.

Fletcher wanted to open his eyes; heaven knew he wanted to, but something stopped him. Something selfish. Something totally alien to his being. Something he had rarely felt before—fear.

What if Aunt Belleville's ecstasy had been misplaced and Beck's gasp had been one of horror? He didn't care! It didn't matter. He loved her; he loved her with all his soul.

But what if Billy, the appealing urchin, had been turned into a weak-willed, simpering miss—and not his Billy Belchem anymore—by the simple application of a bit of lace and ruffles? What if Rosalie had turned beautiful and, now that she'd reacquainted herself with female fripperies, had her sights set on a Season in London, wanting nothing more than to break hearts, enjoying nothing so much as the sight of half a dozen young men dangling at her shoestrings? What if she didn't want him, need him, love him, any more?

"Well, nephew?" Aunt Belleville prompted, preening, her gaze on Rosalie. When Fletcher didn't answer, she looked down on him, only to see that his eyes were still closed. "My goodness, Beck, look! Do you think Fletcher could have been right and they really have stuck that way?"

"Huh?" Beck responded vaguely, all his attention obviously still intent on Rosalie.

His aunt's alarm brought Fletcher back from his brown study. "Why don't you ask me, Aunt? If my eyelids have stuck shut, it does not also stand to reason that I have been rendered deaf." Knowing himself unable to put off the inevitable, he opened his eyes.

His mind felt struck first by the gown, for it had been his gift to Arabella, when his sister had been little more than fourteen. It was a gown of its time, deliberately styled so that the woman who wore it looked helpless and childlike, as if she had just stepped out of bed. The color was butter yellow, the style consisting of a simply cut, modest bosom, tiny puffed sleeves, an émpire waistline accented by trailing yellow velvet ribbon, and a small ruffle at the hem.

It fit Rosalie as if it had been expressly fashioned for her.

The small swell of her breasts had been caught and held; the drape of the fabric followed the gentle flare of her hips, hiding the legs he already knew to be long and straight. Her arms, shown nearly to the shoulder, were soft and white and eminently touchable.

Fletcher swallowed, hard, and raised his gaze to her face.

Rosalie Darley had overnight become the most heart-stoppingly beautiful, most desirable woman he had ever seen.

He didn't know whether he should rejoice or weep. Elsie was indeed a genius. Rosalie's small face sat inside the perfect frame of short, tousled ebony curls run through with a butter-yellow satin ribbon, setting off her small, freckled, upturned nose, pert chin, and enormous emerald eyes.

Her eyes saved him from despair, for they were still the eyes of Billy Belchem—alive, inquiring, mischievous, and somewhat challenging. Billy had not disappeared, he had merely gone into hiding.

"Well, halfling," he said, finding his voice at last, "it seems you clean up rather nicely."

"Nicely?" Beck exploded, getting to his feet to approach Rosalie and kiss her hand. "Miss Darley, with your kind permission I should like to run that odious man through for you. I may hang for it, but it would have been worth it."

"Oh, but you can't do that," Aunt Belleville exclaimed worriedly. "She is affianced to my nephew here, remember, although I suppose you are only funning, aren't you, Beck? Of course you are. I'm all about in my head with excitement."

"We forgive you, Aunt," Fletcher said, rising to kiss her on the cheek. "My compliments, ma'am, for you have indeed wrought a miracle."

Rosalie, who had passed a nearly sleepless night, only to spend the morning being poked and pushed at and fretted over by Elsie and Aunt Belleville, whom she had deemed a nice old tabby for all her fussing and fretting, had heard and seen enough.

It remained one thing to feel pretty again, to be clean

again, to be able to wiggle her toes inside soft slippers, her heavy, chafing boots a thing of the past, but it was an entirely different kettle of fish to be discussed as an object, as if she didn't really exist. Besides, where was the miracle? She knew what she looked like; she'd had eighteen years to become accustomed to her appearance, and she didn't think it to be the slightest bit out of the ordinary.

"If we have done with the inspection," she piped up testily, "do you think it would be possible if this 'miracle' partook of some luncheon?"

Beck all but fell over himself to guide Rosalie to the buffet, pointing out the various dishes as if she would be unfamiliar with them, as she stole a look at Fletcher from beneath her eyelashes.

He still stared at her, a dazed but happy look on his handsome face. Her heart, which she had noticed beating in a rather erratic rhythm ever since Aunt Belleville had positioned her outside the dining room to await her summons, picked up a beat as she tipped her head to hide a smile.

He approved of her! Oh, he might not have rushed to her side to kiss her hand, as Beck had, but it was obvious all the same. He really, really approved of her appearance.

She had been so worried, nearly teased to death, wondering how he would react, for she knew that the same slight body that had made impersonating a young boy so successful must look woefully inadequate dressed in a gown.

Although Aunt Belleville and Elsie had complimented her figure, it had taken the appreciative glint in Fletcher's eyes to assure her that the Beatrices of this world were not necessarily better prepared to attract the attentions of a man—not that Rosalie didn't still covet the barmaid's ample bosom at least a little.

Once seated at the table, Rosalie made a mental note to destroy the letter she had penned to Mrs. Rimston upon arising this morning. Although the woman's kindly worded invitation would be above all things wonderful if Fletcher had rejected her, there no longer existed any need to contemplate yet another escape, yet another masquerade, yet another deception. Truth to tell, Rosalie, who if nothing else had learned from her unintentional lessons at Fletcher's hand, had become most heartily sick of both masquerades and lies.

Of course, she remembered sadly, the matter of Mrs. Beale—and Sawyer—still lingered on like a nagging toothache, a trial to be gotten through before she could believe she had any real chance at lasting happiness with Fletcher.

Fletcher . . . She peeked up at him once more, to see him looking at her, a smile in his soft gray eyes. Dare she hope for a happy ending? Had William, in his final request, reached out to assure a lifetime of happiness for his sister and his best friend?

Halfway through the meal, Beck turned to ask Rosalie if she would honor him by riding out in his curricle that afternoon, only to have Fletcher remind him that, much as he would like to allow it, he had several letters in his study that demanded Beck's immediate attention, and by the by, did his friend recall that Miss Darley had already been spoken for?

"I, on the other hand," he added as Beck blushed and grumbled under his breath, "am delightfully free for the afternoon and would like nothing more than to take Miss Darley up with me while I make a small tour of the estate."

Yes, Rosalie told herself, hiding a triumphant smile behind her serviette, a lifetime of happiness might just be a possibility.

A lovely Kashmir shawl around her shoulders and one of Arabella's feathered bonnets atop her curls, Rosalie relaxed against the wooden seat of the curricle, feeling the smooth fabric of Fletcher's jacket sleeve rubbing comfortingly, provocatively, against her bare arm.

They had been driving for nearly a half-hour in Fletcher's curricle, the same one she had first seen pulling in to the stableyard with Fletcher at the reins, his many-caped driving cloak giving him the appearance of a descending storm cloud. Rosalie remembered how he had hopped down from the seat, barking out orders, and recalled her pert response to those commands.

They had come a long way since that day, and Rosalie did not now believe she regretted a moment they had spent together. Most especially, she knew she would always treasure the night they had shared a meal and a campfire, the night she had heard about William's last hours and learned Fletcher to be, at heart, a wonderful, caring man.

He could also be exasperating, and maddening, and stubborn, and overbearing, and even nasty. But as she knew she had not been exactly honest with him, she could excuse his behavior. Yes, it still rankled that he had subjected her to that scene in his bedchamber, but she also knew, because she had to be nothing else if not honest, that he had been sorely tried, believing himself to be feeling an attraction toward a totally unsuitable *parti*.

And he loved her. Rosalie found a multitude of comfort in that thought, even though Fletcher had not yet confessed as much to her. There were just some things a woman knew, and this was one of them. He could no more deny the softness in his eyes when he looked at her than she could deny the ache in her heart when she caught sight of him.

She had often read of love, of course, as any lover of marble-backed novels had done. She knew there would be trials and troubles—had expected them—but she also knew that, in the end, good always triumphed over evil. Evil, in this case, personified itself not by way of a leering stepfather or a menacing ghost, or even a fire-breathing monster, but by Mrs. Beale and her wretched son, Sawyer.

But Rosalie wasn't afraid—not anymore. Fletcher would slay all her dragons for her, and they would live happily ever after. Aunt Belleville, as that dear woman had already promised a half-dozen times, would help them raise a gaggle of beautiful, well-behaved children in the beauty and peace of Lakeview.

"You're very quiet, halfling," Fletcher remarked, pulling the curricle to a stop beneath a shady tree. "Perhaps you would have preferred we rode out on Pagan and She-Devil?"

"I have no riding habit," she informed him, blushing at the memory of their race and its near-disastrous conclusion.

"It's too late to bar the door, Rosalie, for all your lovely chickens have flown the coop. In other words, I have already seen you ride astride. We could have resurrected the breeches one last time if you had wished it.''

Rosalie shuddered, shaking her head. ''I sincerely hope those breeches have already gone into the fire, as I never wish to see them again. Besides, riding astride has to be the most uncomfortable thing in the world. I don't know how you men endure it.''

Fletcher laughed, hopping down from the seat to tie the reins to a nearby branch. Holding up his hand to her, he bid her to alight, saying that he thought they should walk awhile, so that he might hear more about Mrs. Beale, who could be counted upon to turn up at Lakeview no later than tomorrow afternoon.

Rosalie placed her hand in his, experiencing a thrill of excitement tingle its way to her elbow and beyond, and leapt down lightly from the seat.

''Must we talk about her, Fletcher?'' she asked, lifting her eyes to him in innocent seduction. ''I have already concluded that you shall rout both she and her nasty son without a single problem. You can be very intimidating when you wish to be, you know. William was always far too easy on them, as they are so distantly related that it cannot really signify, and they're nothing but leeches into the bargain, feeding off anyone they feel unable to say no to them.''

''William—cowed by a woman?'' Fletcher asked, tucking Rosalie's hand into the crook of his arm as they walked across the open field toward a small, far-off building that served as a shelter for the sheep in the rain. ''He was a gentle man, I know that, but I can hardly envision him in the role of dupe.''

Tears pricked at the back of Rosalie's eyes as she heard Fletcher speak of her brother. Dear William. She still found it so difficult to remember that he had been lost to her, that she would never see him again.

"William's heart was so pure," she said quietly, placing her other hand on Fletcher's forearm so that she could feel his solid strength with both hands. "He felt he couldn't turn them away when they came to us several years ago and asked for his help. He gave them a small cottage at the edge of the farm, and still they cried poor and asked for more.

"I—" Rosalie's voice broke for a moment before she could continue. "When he insisted that he had a responsibility to his country to join Wellington, I—I made him promise me that he wouldn't die, leaving me with no one save Mrs. Beale as guardian. He laughed and then promised he'd never do that to me. I guess he must have remembered the promise when he had that terrible vision."

She looked up at Fletcher, her eyes swimming in tears. "He wrote to me about the vision in his last letter, the one telling me that he had asked you to become my guardian if anything should happen to him. A few weeks later I learned that he was gone. Did he tell you about the vision?"

Their bodies leaned into each other's as they walked, Fletcher's free hand now lying atop Rosalie's as he told her everything: of William's letter, his own delay in locating it, his anguish, and even his initial reluctance to take on another ward after his tragedy with Arabella.

She had heard parts of this story before, that night in the stable, but Fletcher hadn't been drinking this time, and now his words hit her with twice the impact. He was so sincere, so unwilling to make excuses for himself, that Rosalie felt herself hard-pressed not to stop, fold him into her arms, and comfort him.

Just as she was about to convert thought into action, Fletcher halted, turned to face her, looked deeply into her eyes, and asked, ''Would you like a Season in London, Rosalie? Aunt Belleville seems to think you will take the city by storm, and I am inclined to agree with her.''

''Wh-what?'' He had taken her totally off-guard, and she could only stare up at him in openmouthed amazement.

''No one knows about the happenings of the past days—and no one ever has to know. Your reputation will be safe. All this business of compromise can be buried, with no one to question it. Rosalie, don't just look at me with those wounded green eyes, answer me.''

''You—you don't want me?'' she asked hollowly, her heart dropping to her toes, to lie there with all her shattered, broken dreams.

''Want you?'' Fletcher responded, his voice racked with pain, although Rosalie, caught up in her own misery, did not hear it. ''I read your letter to Mrs. Rimston, halfling.''

Her chin lifted a full two inches. ''You read—you read my letter. How dare you! That was private. Oh, Fletcher, I'm so embarrassed.''

''Why? It was adorably naïve. And now I know you love me—you think you love me. I also know you to be totally innocent, unschooled in the world, and woefully imaginative, not that I don't appreciate the absurd, dramatic workings of your mind. On the contrary, I adore them. But be that as it may, as your guardian I cannot be selfish. I must do what I believe is best for you.''

''Best for me? And you think a Season in London

would be best for me? After what you've told me of the place? I'd be bored to flinders."

"Forget what I said. At the time I said all that I thought I was keeping a young boy from running off to his ruin. London, for a beautiful young lady, constitutes the most wonderful place on earth. Good God, Rosalie, Beck has already closeted himself in his room in order to compose poems to your charms. You will have a hundred suitors. A thousand. How can I possibly tie you to marriage when you have not yet lived?"

"Marriage to you wouldn't be living?" Rosalie retorted, stung into speech. "Never mind, don't answer that. The nail is in, Fletcher, there's no need to hammer it home. You have found yourself amused by me, attracted to me, but you don't really love me. You don't want marriage; you've already made it clear that an escape from clinging women was one of the reasons you returned to Lakeview. Well, I shan't bother you anymore. I will return to Hilltop Farm with Mrs. Beale and Sawyer tomorrow, and let them do what they will with me—Black Mass and all."

"Black Mass?" Fletcher took a step backward, dumbfounded. "Who in blazes told you they were going to use you in a Black Mass? Halfling, that's absurd!"

10

"To think I actually considered marriage to that man. Marriage? To Fletcher Belden? Ha! What a terrible joke! What a completely insane, ridiculous idea! A person would have to be out of her mind, at her last prayers, so firmly on the shelf she was stuck to it, to even consider such folly."

Rosalie all but bounced about her bedchamber in her anger, longing to locate some object that, through the smashing of it, would give her an outlet for her rage, her indignation, her humiliation.

"Black Mass!" Fletcher had chortled, calling her assumption absurd. That was bad enough in itself, but did he have to compound his outburst by leaning himself against a tree trunk to laugh until tears ran down his cheeks? Did he, while wiping at his face with a ridiculously large white handkerchief, have to say in the most unromantic voice she had ever heard, "Black Mass? Oh, Lord, how I adore you, Rosalie," and then go off into another paroxysm of giggles?

Rosalie stopped pacing, her grin impish as she wondered how much he adored her now, after watching her drive off in his curricle, leaving him behind to choke on his mirth.

"It serves him right," she told her disheveled

reflection in the mirror hanging over the dressing table. "The man has done nothing but insult me, trick me, lead me on only to shun me, and laugh at me since the moment we met. How on earth William could have thought him to be a wonderful fellow is entirely beyond my comprehension."

She began to pace once more, but the heat had begun to go out of her anger, for she was at heart a most forgiving person. Biting her bottom lip, she walked to the window, wondering if Fletcher was still waiting for her on the road or if he had begun walking back to Lakeview. "Not that I care so much as a fig," she told herself, lifting her chin to stare up at the ceiling for at least the count of ten while her toe tapped nervously against the carpet.

"Oh, hang him," she exploded at last, scooping up her bonnet once more, and headed for the staircase. "I can't leave the dratted man out there all alone. He'll probably tumble off a cliff or some such stupid thing."

Just as she got to the head of the stairs, there came a loud knocking at the front door and she stepped back a pace, immediately contrite, as she instantly envisioned a farm laborer on the other side of the door, his cap in hand, explaining that he had found Mr. Belden lying broken on the ground, and would anyone want him to fetch home the body.

When Lethbridge opened the door, however, it was not to find a farm laborer standing outside. Oh, no—no indeed.

"You, man! My name is Mrs. Beale. Don't just stand there as if you've been paralyzed. I am to be taken to Mr. Belden at once."

"And me too, Mama, don't forget," a whiny male

voice chirped, immediately setting Rosalie's teeth on edge.

"It's them," Rosalie whispered, one hand to her throat. She prudently backed away from the staircase, whirled about, and ran for her bedchamber, locking the door behind her, to look about the room once more—not for an object to break, but for a possible means of escape.

How dare the Beales arrive a day early? How dare Fletcher be out walking the countryside when they arrived, leaving her to deal with them alone?

No, she wouldn't be alone. Aunt Belleville was here, as was Beck.

Her shoulders slumped. Aunt Belleville and Beck? What could she be thinking of, to believe that either of them could hold out against the bombastic Beales? "Face it, Rosalie," she said on a groan. "You're alone."

Cudgeling her brain for some delaying tactic, some plan to keep herself safe from the Beales until Fletcher returned, Rosalie saw the nightgown Elsie must have brought into the room for her and then laid on the bed.

Stripping to her shift, her gown hastily kicked into a corner, Rosalie dived into the nightgown and had just settled herself beneath the covers when there came a knock at the door.

"Yoo-hoo, Rosalie, are you in there?" Aunt Belleville's voice came through the door even as the doorknob turned a fraction before stopping. "Rosalie, dear, the door seems to be stuck. May I come in? Mrs. Beale is here to see you."

"I—I have the headache," Rosalie called out weakly,

unfortunately too weakly for Aunt Belleville to hear her fib through the door.

"What, dear?"

Rosalie pulled a face. "I have the headache," she called a bit louder.

"You have what?" Clearly Aunt Belleville still had not heard her. "Lethbridge," Rosalie heard the woman call. "Lethbridge, I think something is wrong. Miss Darley has somehow gotten herself locked in her chamber and can't come to the door. Perhaps we should break it down?"

"Oh, good grief," Rosalie groaned, about to rise and unlock the door before remembering Hedge's warning to never, under any circumstances, allow Aunt Belleville to suspect she might be ill. "Dose yer good, she will, with terrible, nasty stuff," Hedge had said, and the expression on his face had been enough to convince Rosalie of the wisdom of the man's words. She might complain of not feeling well, but she was not about to let the woman in to see for herself.

"I have the headache," she all but shouted from the relative safety of her bed, the words no longer a complete lie. If Fletcher didn't get back soon to rescue her, she wouldn't be surprised if she developed the stomachache as well.

"That's not all that's going to ache, halfling, if you don't get yourself down to the yellow saloon in precisely thirty minutes. Your devil-worshipers have come for their human sacrifice, not that I'll let them have you. If anyone is going to snap your lovely neck, it will be me—most probably as a gift on the fiftieth anniversary of our wedding. Until then, I shall do my utmost to restrain myself. Rosalie, do you understand me?"

Fletcher! Rosalie collapsed against the pillows in relief. She didn't know how he had done it, but he must have been able to get a lift back to Lakeview . . . just in time to save her. She smiled dreamily. Wasn't it just like her dearest Fletcher to be there when she needed him, even if he could not resist making fun of her?

"Yes, Fletcher," she called out joyously, sure he would hear her. She threw back the covers and ran to rescue her gown from the corner, hoping it would not need to be pressed, for it was the only gown she possessed. "I'll be prompt, I promise."

Rosalie held the gown in front of her and danced around the room, her fears flown. Fletcher would protect her, even if he made no bones about letting her know he thought her to be a bacon-brained twit. Fletcher loved her.

Aunt Belleville, whose acquaintances would have sworn the woman could not say boo to a goose, felt herself beginning to believe she would like nothing better than to slap Mrs. Beale silly.

She had been sitting across the tea tray from the woman for nearly a half-hour now, and Mrs. Beale hadn't stopped speaking for a moment.

"And so I say to you, Miss Belleville," Mrs. Beale was saying now, her bloodless lips barely moving, "can you blame me for being overset? The girl has shown herself to be a snake in the bosom, a heartless creature, to have run off, leaving us distraught and nearly without the funds needed to launch a search for her. I think she's deranged, if you want my honest opinion, and I have already made inquiries with the local madhouse to have her put away."

"Then she won't be marrying me?" Sawyer Beale broke in from his seat beside his mother. "But, Mama, you promised me, right after we heard about William—although, come to think of it, Rosie always has hated me."

"Shut up, Sawyer," his mother ordered shortly, upon which Sawyer shut his mouth, his lower lip beginning to tremble.

Aunt Belleville looked toward the hallway, praying for her nephew to appear and rescue her before she did the Beale woman an injury. "We have seen no sign of insanity in Rosalie," she put in weakly, thinking about the way Rosalie had looked the first time she had seen her. Was it insane to dress in boy's clothing and sleep in a stable? Perhaps some people might believe it to be so, but Aunt Belleville much preferred to think of Rosalie as an eccentric. She liked the girl, for one thing, and for another, she could not make herself useful tending Fletcher's childen if Rosalie were proven to be just a tad dotty and he was to remain a bachelor.

"Not insane, Miss Belleville?" Mrs. Beale challenged. "And what would you call running off in the dead of night, leaving your only family behind, to traipse alone through the district, falling afoul of only God knows what devilment? She has undoubtedly been ruined by now, which is why I will no longer agree to give my blessing to any marriage between the girl and Sawyer. I will not have my son bedding down with soiled goods."

Aunt Belleville's eyes widened as a great fury enveloped her. A lady she might be, polite she might be—but enough was enough! "Now see here, Mrs. Beale," she retorted hotly, "I feel I must take umbrage with what you are implying, by Jupiter, and I must tell you, ma'am, I can be exceedingly disagreeable when I put my mind to it."

"That she can, Mrs. Beale," Fletcher agreed softly from the doorway, unable to stand outside and listen to any more of this nonsense, the even tone of his voice effectively capturing the attention of everyone in the room. " 'By Jupiter,' Aunt? I didn't know you had it in you. I may yet reconsider the idea of a gilt ceiling for the music room. Bless you, Aunt, but please don't put yourself into a taking. I am here now."

Fletcher walked into the room, his quick scrutiny measuring the Beales against his mental picture of them. They were not, either singularly or collectively, a sight to inspire poetry.

He looked at and dismissed Sawyer in a heartbeat. Young, overdressed, and sadly lacking in both shoulder and chin, Sawyer registered in Fletcher's mind as no more than a bloodless extension of his black crow of a mother, who most assuredly considered herself firmly in charge of everything, from what her son ate to whether he crossed his legs at the knee or the ankle.

Mrs. Beale, on the other hand, presented at least an interesting if not a particularly pleasing sight, reminding Fletcher of a full moon on a coal-black night. Her immense black-clad body represented the night, and her chalk-white face, so full cheeked that her eyes appeared punched into it, likes raisins in a pudding, had to be the moon.

Fletcher tipped his head to one side, measuring Rosalie's charges against Mrs. Beale's appearance. Yes, it was possible to believe this woman capable of holding a Black Mass. He doubted it highly, but it was possible.

In any event, he couldn't fault Rosalie for wishing to put as much space between herself and the Beales as humanly possible, and he made a mental note to congratulate her on her daring.

"Mrs. Beale, I presume? A thousand apologies for keeping you waiting," he said after a moment, bowing in front of the woman. "Allow me to welcome you to Lakeview and to thank you for your timely response to my request to come here. I trust the journey did not prove too arduous?"

Mrs. Beale's reply to his carefully calculated question, as lengthy as it promised to be boring, gave Fletcher the time he needed to formulate a plan to get himself and Rosalie shed of the overstuffed beldame and her muckworm son as soon as possible and with the minimum of fuss.

"Yes, yes, indeed," Fletcher answered vaguely as Mrs. Beale's voice finally ground down, knowing that all such a woman wanted in life was someone who would agree with her. "And you—Sawyer, isn't it?—how did you fare on the road?" he asked, turning to the younger man to survey him through the lense of his chased-silver quizzing glass.

Sawyer, Fletcher could see, had been as impressed by Fletcher's carefully selected dove-colored pantaloons, silver-buttoned coat of superfine, finely starched cravat, and spotless waistcoat as he had been intended to be. "The cheese was bad at the inn we stopped at," Sawyer whined absently, for he did not know how to speak without whining. "I say, Mr. Belden, that cravat's a masterpiece. Slap up to the mark!"

Fletcher grinned down at the young man, who hadn't

risen to shake his hand. "I try," he answered humbly, turning back to Mrs. Beale. "Do I have your permission to sit, ma'am?"

"You have my permission to fetch Rosie to me as soon as possible, so that we might be on our way back to Patterdale. You do have her, don't you?"

"Does anyone ever really 'have' anyone else, ma'am?" Fletcher questioned philosophically, neatly crossing one leg over the other at the knee, because it was his choice to do so. "I mean, you must have thought you had her, but like a little bird, she flew away, only to light down here, at Lakeview. How can I be assured that you could keep her, if you were to 'have' her again?"

"Fletcher," Aunt Belleville exclaimed, aghast. "Surely you don't plan to hand dear Rosalie over to this horrid woman, do you?"

"That's a good question, ma'am, and one I too would delight in hearing answered, as it would appear your nephew changes his mind as often as he changes his clothes."

"Rosie! My hopes were quite cut up!" Sawyer leapt to his feet, his thin body quivering, whether with delight or with dread only he knew. He took two steps forward, and Fletcher audibly cleared his throat. Sawyer stopped in his tracks, looked down at his feet as if asking them what they thought they were doing, then subsided once more into his chair.

Fletcher's nonverbal threat did not so intimidate Mrs. Beale, who quickly launched into speech. "There you are, you heartless girl. Come here at once so that I might look at you. That had better not be rouge I see on those cheeks."

"Rouge," Aunt Belleville choked out, taking the woman's words as a personal insult. "I'll have you know, Mrs. Beale, that no child in my charge has ever worn rouge. And to think I had felt sorry for you. It's no wonder poor Rosalie ran off. I would do likewise, had I been her."

"Exactly right, Aunt Belleville," Rosalie agreed, joining her champion on the settee, to put a protective arm about the woman's shoulders. "Mrs. Beale, that was a most insulting remark, and I demand you apologize to Miss Belleville at once."

"Apologize?" Mrs. Beale sputtered, her three chins beginning to wobble. "I'll do no such thing, you impertinent chit. I won't take any sauce from you, girl, or any orders either."

"Ladies, ladies, please, can't we talk reasonably?" Fletcher interposed, rising between the women before they could come to blows. Things had been going so well until Rosalie had joined them. He had taken the Beales' measure and had been about to offer them what they wanted—money—in exchange for Mrs. Beale's cooperation in settling the matter to everyone's satisfaction. Now, thanks to Rosalie, and his aunt's unexpected display of venom, there was nothing else for it but to go dragging through the entire guardianship question. "Surely there is no need for dramatic confrontation?"

Three sets of female eyes were now riveted in Fletcher's direction, and he found himself wilting fractionally under the strain.

"She insulted me, nephew," Aunt Belleville complained, pouting.

"You have no right, sirrah," Mrs. Beale challenged gruffly.

"Oh, go put your head under the pump, Fletcher," Rosalie groused in a less-than-loverlike tone.

And with that the three ladies were off again, arguing nineteen to the dozen, until Fletcher longed to clap his hands over his ears.

He had tried to be good. He had tried to be fair. He had, as a gentleman of the world, attempted to settle a ticklish matter with a minimum of fuss, protecting Rosalie's reputation while at the same time putting an effective period to any of Mrs. Beale's claims to guardianship over the woman he loved—the "delicately nurtured" young woman who had just told him to go soak his head.

He felt tempted, most sorely tempted, to quit the room and leave the three of them behind to tear one another's hair out at the roots, winner take all. But he called himself a gentleman and he couldn't opt for the lower road in that way. It fell to him to restore some sort of order to the conversation, and he knew of only one way to do it.

Taking a deep breath, he announced importantly, "May I have your attention, please? Ladies, Mr. Beale? Thank you. William Darley left his sister, Rosalie, in my charge, naming me as her guardian until such time as she marries or comes of age. I have a letter to that effect—duly witnessed and depressingly legal—in my possession. As I plan to wed Miss Darley within the week—against her will if necessary, I might add—it would appear that I am to be not only the executor of William's wishes but also the means through which his wishes will be accomplished. Now, have I satisfied everybody here, or am I going to have to get nasty?"

"You were wonderful!"

"Yes, I was, wasn't I?" Fletcher leaned down to kiss the top of Rosalie's head, glorying in this high praise.

Rosalie snuggled more deeply into Fletcher's embrace as they sat close together on the settee, the rest of the household already in bed for the night. "I thought Mrs. Beale would have an apoplexy, but she seemed to accept William's letter at last. What choice did she have, really, with you all but daring her to disagree with you?" She turned her head to look up at him. "You can be very masterful, you know."

Fletcher grinned, liking the thought that his betrothed considered him to be masterful almost as much as he reveled in the knowledge that she believed him to be wonderful. "And have you at last allowed yourself to be convinced that she had only planned for you to marry her wretched Sawyer and harbored no plan to involve you in a Black Mass?"

Rosalie blushed, averting her head. "Oh, do be quiet. How was I to know what they were doing, skulking around out of doors at midnight, making those strange noises?" she protested feebly. She kicked off her slippers, to pull her legs up under her on the settee. "I didn't even know Sawyer had a cat, yet alone that he had lost it. And you have to admit it, Mrs. Beale looks capable of anything."

"The woman's a born antidote, all right," Fletcher agreed happily enough, beginning to play with an errant curl that hung down over Rosalie's left ear. "Mrs. Beale," he murmured reflectively. "Does she have a first name?"

Rosalie shrugged, then giggled. "I asked Sawyer one time, thinking I should be calling her Aunt Something-or-other, but he just looked at me in that vacant way of his, as if he didn't understand the question. Personally, I think he believes her name is Mama. What a turnip head!''

''And to think that you have given up the chance to be Mrs. Turnip Head.''

Rosalie gave him a playful punch in the stomach. ''Now that's nasty, Fletcher,'' she protested, although her heart wasn't in it. She felt too happy to be angry with anyone.

She wasn't angry with Mrs. Beale, who had blustered and fumed and then relented when Fletcher had told her she could have the cottage she and her son already occupied and a small yearly allowance, or she could go to perdition for all he cared, it made no never-mind to him. She couldn't even find it in herself to be angry with Sawyer, who had made one last attempt to win her affections by promising to love her very much if she took him to London, before she threatened to do him an injury and he had retreated behind his mama's ample black skirts.

As a matter of fact, with the bombastic Beales already on the way back to their cottage, hopefully never to be seen or heard from again, Rosalie could even find it in her heart to remember them with at least a little charity.

For Fletcher loved her, and Rosalie was in charity with the whole world.

''Halfling?'' Fletcher prompted, bringing her out of her reverie.

''Hmm?'' she breathed, too deliciously comfortable to move.

''I have something for you.''

She was immediately alert. Sitting up on her knees,

she threw her arms tightly around his neck, for she was a demonstrative person and Fletcher had already proved to her that he appreciated her impulsive displays of affection. "What is it, my love? Tell me! Will I like it?"

Fletcher disentangled himself from his affectionate fiancée in order to reach in his pocket and draw out a small velvet case with a large "B" fashioned on it in gilt script. "You will lead me a dog's life, imp," he said not unhappily, "but I think I will be able to bear up under the strain if you promise to hug me like that a minimum of ten times a day. Now, please be serious for a moment, for I am about to propose marriage, and if I am interrupted, I may forget what I am doing and we will never get to the altar."

The time for levity, for delicious stolen kisses and shared laughter, was over. Fletcher was being deadly serious, even if his tone was light.

Rosalie bit at her bottom lip, eyeing the case apprehensively. It held the Belden family ring, she was sure of it, and she felt a quick stab of anxiety as she wondered if she could really believe herself truly worthy of it. She was such a zany, so prone to flights of the imagination, so apt to act on impulse and think later.

If it hadn't been for a tremendous run of good luck, she would never have even reached Lakeview in the first place. By rights, her limp, broken body should have been found along the road, the victim of foul play. Not only that, but just the thought of the misadventures she had participated in—and even instigated—since meeting Fletcher was enough to prompt her to believe that the best thing she could do for all concerned would be to cry off this betrothal and, like disgraced ladies of old, get herself to a nunnery. If the good sisters would take her, that is.

She looked deeply into Fletcher's eyes, laying her hand on the case in order to keep it closed. "Are you sure, Fletcher? Are you very, very sure?"

Fletcher put his hand over hers, steadily returning her gaze. "I was struck by you the moment I first saw you. I lusted after you when I still believed you to be a lad—much as it pains me to say that. Discovering your true identity made me the happiest, although equally the most beleaguered, man in the world. My whole heart, my whole mind, wants nothing more out of life than to have you by my side through eternity, surprising me with your flights of fancy, confounding me with your penchant for mischief, driving me to the edge of madness with your innocent insanity, and generally making mice feet of my existence.

"I also want to marry you because I truly believe I could not exist without your love, your bright smile, your warm body snuggled next to mine, our babies at your breast. Rosalie, my darling halfling, take my ring, please. Take my life, it's yours. I love you so much I ache with it."

Rosalie's tears flooded her eyes before spilling over to run down her cheeks. She raised her hands to gently cup Fletcher's dear face. "No wonder William gave me to you. He must have known it would end like this. Yes, my darling, I'll take your ring—and in return I'll give you my heart."

Epilogue

"He seems happy, doesn't he?" Rosalie asked as she and Fletcher paused at the first turning in the lane to wave back at Beck as he stood in the open front door of Hilltop Farm, his arm around his wife of three weeks. "And Betsy is a lovely woman."

Fletcher looked over at his own wife, her slim body clad in a fashionably cut midnight-blue velvet riding habit as she sat atop She-Devil. She was even more beautiful now than she had been two years earlier, on their wedding day, and he believed he loved her even more now than he had then.

"And why shouldn't he be happy, halfling?" he asked as they turned their horses to begin a leisurely ride to the inn that would be their first stop on the way back to Lakeview. "Poor Beck was nearly delirious over your extremely generous wedding present of the deed to the farm."

Rosalie turned to look at her husband. "You didn't mind, did you? I mean, Beck has been managing the farm for us and . . . Well, I just felt it was right that he have something of his own. He's a wonderful man and a good friend."

"And you wanted to pay him back for being gentleman enough to volunteer to manage Hilltop after our marriage, knowing full well that the fellow believed himself to be half in love with you. Now, if I could only bring Lethbridge to voicing his intentions concerning my aunt, I should think everyone would be happy,'' Fletcher teased lightly.

''Wretch,'' Rosalie said in much the same tone she said ''darling,'' something she did quite often; nearly as often as Fletcher addressed her as ''halfling.'' She raised her chin an inch. ''Besides, I have it from Aunt Belleville that things are progressing quite nicely, thank you.''

They rode on in companionable silence, enjoying the awesome beauty of the Lake District in the spring, stopping to watch the lapwings perform their incredible acrobatics, listening to the lowing of the cows, taking in the delicious aroma of wildflowers that perfumed the air.

It had been several months since they had taken their last ride through the district, Rosalie's pregnancy keeping them from what had—over the protests of Aunt Belleville, who thought the exercise extremely odd—become their favorite entertainment. Rosalie rode sidesaddle now, having vowed never to wear breeches again, but they still spent an occasional night sleeping under the stars, although they shared their blankets now and they didn't get that much sleep.

''I hope Aunt Belleville isn't having too much trouble with William,'' Rosalie said hours later as they sat in a private dining parlor at the inn, her green eyes dreamy as she thought of her young son. ''I think he might be cutting another tooth.''

''Lethbridge is there with her, darling, as well as Elsie,'' Fletcher reminded her, taking Rosalie's hand

and leading her toward the staircase. "Willie will be fine, I promise you."

Rosalie shook her head. "Don't call him Willie, Fletcher. He doesn't look like a Willie."

Opening the door to their bedchamber without letting go of his wife's hand, Fletcher conjured up a mental picture of his son, a chubby cherub with hair as dark as midnight and a huge pair of intelligent green eyes. "You're right, halfling, he doesn't look like a Willie. He looks like a Billy. He looks exactly like my Billy Smith-Belchem."

Rosalie pulled her hand away and began unbuttoning the jacket of her riding habit. "I suppose," she said, smiling at her husband, "you will never let me forget that unfortunate misunderstanding?"

"Never. The memory is too enjoyable." Stretching out across the bed, Fletcher patted the space beside him and teased, "Join me?"

Rosalie slipped out of her divided skirt and approached the bed, her smile softly seductive. She looked at him and frowned. "But your boots, Fletcher. What about your boots?"

Fletcher grinned wickedly, raising one leg. "Halfling, I thought you'd never ask."

About the Author

Michelle Kasey is the pseudonym of Kasey Michaels, which is the pseudonym of Kathie Seidick, a suburban Pennsylvania native who is also a full-time wife and the mother of four children. Her love of romance, humor, and history combine to make Regency novels her natural medium.

A Difficult Disguise continues the story of Fletcher Belden begun in *Midnight Masquerade*, and Lord Bourne's story is told in *The Beleaguered Lord Bourne*, the first in a Michelle Kasey trilogy for Signet that also includes *The Toplofty Lord Thorpe* and *The Ruthless Lord Rule.*